I0580035

DAVID NETH

HEAT

THE GATEKEEPER

BOOK 3

DN Publishing

The Gatekeeper
Heat, Book 3
Copyright © 2019 by David Neth
Batavia, NY

www.DavidNethBooks.com

ISBN: 978-1-945336-68-3
First edition

Subscribe to the author's newsletter for updates and exclusive content:
DavidNethBooks.com/Newsletter

Follow the author at:
www.facebook.com/DavidNethBooks
www.instagram.com/dneth13

DN Publishing

ALSO BY DAVID NETH

HEAT
BLACK MAGNET

DUST STORM

THE GATEKEEPER

FUSE
ORIGIN

OMERTÀ

OBLIVION

UNDER THE MOON
THE FULL MOON

THE HARVEST MOON

THE BLOOD MOON

THE CRESCENT MOON

THE BLUE MOON

THE ART OF MAGIC

STANDALONE
ALL I EVER WANTED

CHAPTER ONE
DETECTIVE HARKNESS

One small coffee, please." Detective Jenna Harkness rolls up her car window after ordering in the drive-thru lane. The nights have been getting chilly and it hasn't quite warmed up yet this morning. She pulls up to the next window and pays before taking her cup, specifically marked "HOT," and placing it securely in the center cupholder before merging back onto the street.

Traffic isn't too bad as she finishes her commute to the police station downtown. It helps that she doesn't have to cross any bridges along her way. There are six of them that cross the river, four of which are downtown. It never seems to be enough for the rush hour drivers, though, which makes her grateful that her commute to the police station is relatively painless.

After showing her badge to security, she pulls into the parking garage under the station and finds one of the reserved spots to park her black Honda. It's nothing special—she doesn't need anything fancy—but it's fast when she needs it to be.

Upstairs, she takes a careful sip of her coffee as she steps into the open office.

"Good morning," she says to Detective Walter Watkins.

"Morning," he grumbles.

Setting her cup down on her desk, she hits the power button to her computer and gets settled into her chair.

"D'you see that Lawson's already bringing in the crazies this morning?" he asks from behind his desk a few feet away from Harkness's. He nods across the room.

Harkness looks over to one of the desks near the window. Officer Lawson is filling out paperwork. Across from him sits a dirty middle-aged man with greasy gray hair and a scruffy beard of the same color. His brown flannel shirt sits open, revealing a stained beige T-shirt underneath with a small hole forming in the corner of the shirt pocket. Rocking back and forth, he murmurs to himself, his eyes not focusing on anything specific.

"What's that about?" Harkness asks Watkins.

He shrugs. "Who knows? Probably public intoxication or something minor. Either way, he's weird."

"Hmm." She turns her attention back to her computer and logs into her email. Updates on various criminal cases, time sheet reminders, and event invites all litter her inbox, which had been cleared Friday evening when she left for the day. As she does every morning, but especially on Mondays, she begins the process of deleting all the irrelevant ones.

"You have a nice weekend?" Watkins asks.

"Yeah, I guess," she says. "Nothing special. The highlight was probably that I got caught up on paperwork."

"You need to get out, Harkness," Watkins says. "You're young! Live while you can still move!"

She smiles politely and returns to her emails. The thirty years Watkins has put into the force shows in his creaky joints, graying hair, and vast amount of wrinkles. Quite the contrast to Harkness's youthful appearance, which to her has always felt like a detriment to her credibility as a detective. That, and the fact that she's a woman.

Officer Lawson steps out of the office into the break room, apparently fed up with the progress he's making with the "crazy," as Detective Watkins so lovingly called him. Curious to know the story, Harkness decides her coffee needs an extra sugar and carries it into the break room where, thankfully, Lawson is alone. He's leaning up against the counter playing on his phone while he waits for the coffee to fill.

"Rough morning already?" she asks, shaking a pink packet of sweetener.

"You don't even know."

Lawson is about the same age as Harkness. Took a few extra years for him to get into the police program than her, which is part of the reason he's still in uniform. From the few times she's talked to him, Harkness knows that he's a genuinely nice guy. And attractive. His dark features accent his strong jaw, which helps him be intimidating with people when he needs to be. Something that Harkness has always been a little bit envious of. But all-in-all they have a good working relationship. Perhaps he could even be someone that she could spend some of her weekends with, per Watkins' suggestion.

"Anything I can help with?" she fishes.

Lawson rolls his eyes. "Not unless you can find that man his meds, which he's clearly forgotten to take. He thinks it's still 1969!"

Her eyebrows shoot up, but she maintains eye contact with her coffee, mixing in the extra sweetener slowly. "*Does* he now…"

"Yeah. He wouldn't believe me when I told him it's 2019." He pulls out a Styrofoam cup and fills it from the carafe.

"Where'd you find this guy?" Cradling her own cup, she sips it slowly and glances at him. Hopefully she can use her own unique charms to wiggle some extra details out of him. Not that it's ever worked for her before.

"Over at Riverside Park. Our guy apparently ran up to a woman jogging and 'freaked out,' as she put it. When she tried to brush him off he grabbed her and wouldn't let go. Someone else saw it and called it in."

"Scary."

"What's scary is that this guy doesn't know what he was doing in the park, how he got there, or where he lives. He's a nutcase."

With the confines of her reality recently expanded, Harkness asks, "Do you mind if I try to talk to him? Maybe he'll respond better to a woman."

Lawson looks out the door, considering it. "He assaulted a woman this morning, Jenna."

"The building is filled with police officers, what's the worst he's going to do?"

He sighs. "Okay. But be careful."

"Just take a seat at my desk and keep an eye out if it makes you feel better. It'll be fine." She hates being treated with extra delicacy just because she was a woman. More than once she has proven that she's capable of handling herself.

Back out in the main office, Harkness steps over to Lawson's desk, sensing the number of eyes suddenly on her. She ignores them and turns to the man rocking back and forth. "Do you mind if I sit here?"

He doesn't look at her. Only continues to rock. "It doesn't make sense."

"What doesn't?" she asks.

"I need to get back home."

Harkness takes a seat, still holding her coffee in both hands. "What's your name?" She uses her sweet voice. "Maybe I can help you get back home."

Still rocking, he mutters, "It doesn't make sense."

"What doesn't?" she pushes. "We're only trying to help."

"Joanie is going to miss me."

Chapter One

"Is Joanie your wife?"

At last, he actually responds to her question. "No, daughter."

Smiling, Harkness says, "Okay! Do you want me to call her for you? Could she take you home?"

"No, it doesn't make sense. She needs me. I've gotta get home."

Just as quickly as it came, her smile fades. Instead, she tries something else. "Why don't you tell me what happened in the park? What were you doing there?"

The man's head starts to shake. "I didn't mean to hurt her."

"No, I'm sure you didn't," she says. "I'm sure she's fine. She was just really scared. What did you want to say to her?"

"*I* was scared," he says.

"Scared of what? What's going on?"

For the first time, he turns to her, tears in his eyes, saliva coating his lips, threatening to spill out. "He's going to hurt her!" He slams his bound fists on the desk and rises to his feet.

In an instant, Officer Lawson and Detective Watkins are there, each grabbing an arm of the grubby man.

"Who?" Harkness pushes, ignoring her colleagues and springing to her feet as well. "Who's going to hurt you?"

"That's enough, Jen," Watkins says.

"Let's get you to a nice cozy cell, okay?" Lawson tells the man.

Harkness follows them out. "Who is trying to hurt you?"

"The man!" he shouts as he's dragged toward the elevators. "The man in the leather mask! He's going to kill her! I saw her! You have to help!"

The elevator doors slowly shut, silencing the man's shouts to muffled echoes.

Stunned, Harkness stares at the closed doors as she replays the encounter in her head. Clearly, the man was unstable, but not dangerous. At least, not in an offensive way. From her best judgment, he's only trying to protect his daughter.

Joanie. Wherever she is.

Despite the hasty assessment, Harkness believes Lawson might be right and that this man does need to see a mental health professional. So one of the first orders of business will be to make some phone calls to get him into a psychiatric center as soon as possible. Maybe once he's on the right medication, he'll be more likely to talk.

The next order of business will be to identify and locate Joanie, if she even exists. Perhaps the man is schizophrenic and acting out a scene from his memory. The psychiatrist will be able to determine that for sure. Still, best to be safe than sorry. If Joanie is out there somewhere, Harkness doesn't want to waste any time in finding her.

The thing that gnaws at her most is the mention of the leather mask. Similar to the leather suit that Heat wears. She's almost certain it's not Heat—although, to be honest, she doesn't know him that well. Still, the man never mentioned any flames, not to say that there weren't any or that Heat just decided to cool it during their encounter, all puns aside.

Despite that suspicion, though, she knows that this case is already too weird for the Ellsworth Police Department to handle on their own. Reaching for her phone, she pulls up the right number and anxiously waits as it rings.

Just as it's about to go to voicemail, he picks up, his voice haggard from the early hour. "Hello?"

"Ash, this is Detective Harkness. I might have a case that requires your expertise."

Chapter Two

ASH

"My expertise?" I sit on the edge of the couch, the blanket still wrapped over my legs. With my free hand I try to wipe the sleep out of my eyes. Extending out my legs brings a groan to the back of my throat as my muscles stretch.

"Did I wake you up?" she asks.

"It's okay," I say as an admission. "I slept in too late anyway."

Glancing up, I note that Perry's door is closed. Did he sleep in too? He's going to be late to work.

"Sorry," she says. "You probably don't want to be bombarded with this as soon as you wake up, but you're the only one I know with…well, with this expertise."

"Please don't mind my bluntness so early in the morning, but what are you trying to say?"

"Do you know anyone…of your kind that, uh, wears a leather mask?"

My mind goes instantly to the Gatekeeper. The one we've been searching for since he slipped away when the Ellsworth

Science and Technology Research lab burned down. The one who is indirectly responsible for the deaths of several otherwise innocent people. The one who is somehow all that's left of my family.

"Yeah," I say with a sigh. "I do."

"Great! I need to know who it is. And I need the CliffsNotes version."

"The what?"

"Bullet points! Give me only the pertinent information."

"Well, it's a long story. There isn't really a…cliff version—what was that thing called?"

"CliffsNotes. It's…well, never mind. Right now I need as much information out of you as I can get in the next five to ten minutes. If you could make it two minutes that would be even better."

"You're really putting me on the spot here." The biggest things I wanted to think about this early in the morning was getting to the bathroom before Perry and getting my morning coffee. "Why do you ask?"

"Well, we have someone in here who says that someone in a leather mask is going to hurt his daughter. Or rather, someone he *says* is his daughter. If this person even exists. He doesn't seem the most reliable."

"You're giving this guy a lot of credibility here. What other descriptions did he give for the person in a leather mask?"

"He didn't. Just said that the man in the leather mask was going to hurt her. Some of my coworkers think he's mentally unstable, but he could also just be acting like that because of stress or lack of sleep or…anything, really."

"Yeah, and this guy in the leather mask could just be a copycat now that he's seen me on TV and stuff," I offer as another alternative. "Maybe he thinks that if I can wear a mask, so can he. Only, he's going to use it to threaten people."

"Maybe," she says, disbelievingly. "But I think this guy and his story are still worth checking out. He claims there's a girl at risk here and unless we find concrete evidence that shows that he's lying, we need to proceed as if someone is really in danger."

"Who is this guy who is giving you this story?" I ask.

"Someone who was called in for harassing a woman at Riverside Park."

"Sounds like a stand-up guy."

"There's more to it. I can tell you about it later."

"Did you get a name for the man?"

"No, he got a little, uh, *unruly* and a couple other officers took him down to a cell." Paper ruffles on the other end. "Ah… the arresting officer is calling him a John Doe on his paperwork, so he didn't get a name either."

"Damn. That might help us determine how he could be connected."

"I know. It also poses a problem for me trying to track down his daughter to see if she actually exists and if she's actually in danger."

"So what are you going to do in the meantime?" I run my hands through my matted hair.

"I'm going to try to get him into a psychiatric center and maybe get him on some meds so he's in a better headspace to talk to us."

"Do you think the drugs will work?"

"It'll be better than the responses I'm getting now," she says. "He's in shock, so he's not really saying much. Getting him some treatment should help him."

"Why's he in shock?"

My question is interrupted by another conversation on her end.

"Huh?" Harkness asks someone next to her, the phone temporarily pulled away from her. "Are you sure? Room #4? Okay, give me a minute."

"You there?" she asks a moment later.

"Yeah, still here."

"They're going to bring him up to one of the interview rooms," she says. "The man said he'd talk to me, but *only* me. Looks like I just showed these boys a thing or two about kindness."

"Find out more about the mask and other features of the man who is threatening his daughter," I tell her, realizing I haven't given her any of the information she originally called for. "The man in the leather mask that I know goes by the Gatekeeper. At least, that's what we call him. He wears a trench coat and he's got a bit of a hunch because he's in his seventies."

"In his *seventies*?"

"Yeah. And see if this John Doe witnessed the Gatekeeper doing anything…super. He can create portals out of thin air. They look like giant balls of light. He's the one who started the fire storm in the city back in July."

"That was *him*? I should write this stuff down." On the other end, Harkness sorts through various writing utensils that clatter against the pencil holder and rings in Ash's ears.

"We haven't figured out what exactly the Gatekeeper wants yet, but he certainly hates me," I go on. "And he knows my name, so if that comes up it's probably him."

"Your real name or…?"

"Real name. It's a long story."

"Sounds like it." Through the phone, I can hear her tapping her pen on a pad of paper. "Actually, would you mind just coming down here? You can sit in on the other side of the interview room and see if you recognize him or if you pick up on anything else he might say. Maybe it's a clue I'd overlook."

"When are you going to interview him?"

She clears her throat. "Uh…now."

"Oh wow, okay." I glance up at the clock on the wall. "Um… I'll be there as soon as I can. Maybe half hour or so?"

"Okay," she says slowly with a sigh. Clearly, she doesn't like my answer. It's already a later start to the morning than I was expecting to get. "I'll stall until then. Third floor. Let someone know you're coming to sit in on the interview. They'll bring you right in."

"All right, I'll hurry."

"Thank you so much."

"No problem, thanks for calling. See you in a bit."

After I hang up the phone, I rub my face in my hands. That phone call has already made it a long morning and I haven't even gotten out of bed yet. Well, what I consider my bed: Perry's living room couch. Hopefully it's not a sign of how the day is going to proceed but I don't have high hopes.

The sound of the toilet flushing in the bathroom pulls me out of my head. My eyes snap up to Perry's bedroom door, which is still shut tight. When did someone else get in here? Slowly, I rise to my feet and step toward the bathroom door, waiting for whoever is inside to exit.

The next moment, a short brunette walks out in one of Perry's T-shirts and not much else. With her head down, she nearly collides with me and screams when she sees me. Perry whips open his door a second later and she runs right into him as she tries to escape back into the bedroom, slamming the door behind her.

"What happened?" His eyes are slits from the rising morning sun.

"I didn't know she spent the night!"

Violet Harrison, the one Perry's been dating for the last month. She works in one of the administrative offices at Ellsworth Institute of Technology, where he is also employed. They've been acting like lovesick teenagers ever since they got together. I thought I had a night off from the sap, but I guess I was wrong.

He gives me a bashful smile before looking down at the floor. "Yeah, last night was the first night we—"

"Perry, I *swear*, if you say *another word!*" Violet shouts from the other side of the door.

He gives another smile in an attempt to feign embarrassment but instead boasts his own blend of masculine pride.

"Dude, I was right outside!" I yell back at him.

"You didn't hear anything!" He pauses, then asks, "Did you?"

"Perry, would you *shut! Up!*" she shouts.

"No, I didn't hear anything!" I say, more for her benefit than for his. "But it doesn't matter! That's—you—just *warn* me next time and I'll stay away."

He shrugs. "Sorry. I just thought since it's technically my apartment..."

I let out a heavy sigh and scratch my forehead. I can't be too mad at him because I'm a guest here just as much as Violet is. The only difference is, I wasn't the one who got an embarrassing wake-up call.

"It's just...gross."

"Sorry," he repeats, then lowers his voice and steps closer to me. "For what it's worth, though, I don't think she will want to come over again when you're here."

"Don't think that I'm not listening!" she shouts from the other side of the door.

He offers a cringing grin.

I roll my eyes and let out a deep breath. "It doesn't matter right now. I need to get going. Detective Harkness called and wants me to sit in on an interview."

"An interview? For what? Is this about you being an informant?"

I glare at him, trying to convey to him that he should heed Violet's advice and shut up.

"Yes. Someone who...someone who might be connected to a case I have some information on."

He nods, finally taking the hint. "That's good. When do you need to get down there?"

Chapter Two

"Like…now."

"Oh."

"Yeah," I say. "Hence, why I needed to get in the bathroom before I ran into our unexpected visitor." I raise my voice and turn to Perry's door. "Sorry about that, Vie!"

"It's okay." Her voice is small, nearly inaudible. I don't think me talking about it helped the situation any.

"All right, well let's get going then." He motions back to his room. "I'll…I'll just, uh…just give me a minute."

We turn away from each other, but a thought hits me. "Wait, aren't you supposed to be at work?"

He stops, his hand on the doorknob. "Normally, yes. We each took the morning off in case we wanted…breakfast."

"Gross." I make a face and turn away, but another thought strikes me. "But you're still going into work then, right?"

"I was planning on leaving in the next hour or so. That's why I got up."

"Do you mind leaving sooner so you can give me a ride?"

He sighs, clearly disappointed. "Yeah, I suppose. I think this morning is pretty well ruined already."

"Sorry about that." I look up at the clock again. "Well, let's get a move on. I need to be at the police station in fifteen minutes!"

Chapter Three

ASH

Perry drops me off at the front of the police station downtown. Traffic is a mess with commuters trying to get to work. Men and women dressed in business attire march up and down the sidewalk on a mission to get to their office with as little human interaction as possible. Car horns beep from the next street over and the grumble of a loud exhaust radiates from the oversized truck waiting at the intersection at the corner.

The merry sounds of a downtown morning.

As I climb out of the back seat of Perry's car, he calls to me over the roar of the outside noise, "Are you going to need a ride home too?"

"No, I'll catch a bus." Casting a wave in their direction on my way up the front steps, I add, "Thanks for the ride! See you later!"

Violet sat in the passenger seat the whole way here, not a single word spoken to anyone. Not that I can blame her after what happened this morning. And that's not to mention her

Chapter Three

needing to get ready early—and in a hurry—on her morning off so that Perry could give me a ride. I haven't really talked to her much but I know one thing for certain: we're definitely not starting things off on the right foot.

They've only been dating for about a month so I know he hasn't told her the specifics of our arrangement. From her point of view, I look like a freeloader. Which I guess I am, to a point. I need to find another job so I can at least pay him *something* for rent. That would alleviate some of this guilt I'm carrying around.

Through the front doors of the police station, I step into the marble-clad lobby and make my way to the group of people hovering near the elevators. Checking the time on my phone again, I see it's already been a half hour since Harkness called. She's probably already started the interview, which means I'm missing it. The odds have been stacked against me this morning, with each step forward presenting a new obstacle along the way. Hopefully this bad luck streak doesn't continue.

Finally, the elevator doors slide open and several people step off, allowing me and the rest of the group of people to pile in. It isn't until the doors close that it occurs to me that it probably would've been faster to take the stairs. Checking my phone again, I see more time tick away until graciously, the doors open on the correct floor and allow me to pass.

Finding the nearest person in uniform, I tell them, "Detective Harkness called and wanted me to observe an interview she's doing. Do you know where to find her?"

The uniform leads me down the hall to a door with a sign hanging that reads, "OBSERVATION ROOM #4 - INTERVIEW IN PROGRESS." Looks like she *did* get started without me. Not that I can blame her.

Inside, the transcriber sits at the counter closest to the window overlooking the interview room. Beside the door sits a man in a uniform, watching Detective Harkness and Detective Watkins talk to the man through the window. Taking a seat in the only open chair in the room, I try to catch up on what I've missed.

The audio is quiet and from my vantage point I don't get a very clear view of the man, but I can already tell that I don't know him. At least, not that I remember. Middle-aged, dirty, gray straggly hair. I rack what little memories I have to try to connect him with family, friends, former teachers, even relatives, but I come up empty.

"Your witness is here," the transcriber says quietly into a mic when he sees me.

After a minute, Harkness gets up and excuses herself from the room, opening the door to the observation room a few seconds later.

She gives a sidelong glance to the officer sitting in the corner, then asks me, "What do you think?"

I shake my head.

"Hmm." She looks through the glass as Watkins continues to talk to the man. "Turn up the volume, would you? We can barely hear anything."

The transcriber adjusts a knob and Watkins' voice rings out louder from the speakers on the ceiling.

"…help you if you talk to us," he says in a soft tone that sounds fake, probably because it is. "If you don't say anything, we're going to have to go strictly with the facts: you were assaulting that woman. As for your alleged daughter, we have no reason—other than your word—to believe that she's in any sort of trouble."

"Let me talk to the lady cop," the man says. "I'll only talk to her."

"Yeah, he wouldn't say much with both of us in the room," Harkness tells me.

"How long have you been in there?" I ask.

"Maybe ten minutes." She watches Watkins and the man with her arms crossed and determination on her face. "I stalled

Chapter Three

as long as I could."

"Sorry," I murmur.

"We can't allow that," Watkins tells the man. "Not with the circumstances in which you were arrested."

"I didn't mean to hurt her!" he says. "Please, let me talk to her."

"Why the fascination with you?" I ask her.

"Maybe because I was the only one who was nice to him." She glances over her shoulder to the officer. "Lawson picked him up."

With a nod, I catch Lawson's unhappy stare from the corner. Looks like Harkness took over his case.

"What has he said so far?"

"Just restated what he said earlier—oh, and I don't think I told you, he thinks it's 1969."

My eyebrows go up. "Interesting."

"'Crazy' is more like it," Lawson says.

"My request to get him into a psychiatric center is still being processed," Harkness explains to me. "I figured getting him in there and talking to him would be better than—where did Watkins go?"

As if he heard his name, the other detective emerges through the door behind Harkness, stepping into the cramped observation room.

"He's not telling me anything." With a groan, he takes a seat next to the transcriber. "Keeps insisting on talking to you, Miss Lead Detective."

Harkness repositions to address the whole room. "Maybe I should just talk to him then."

"Don't be stupid," Watkins says. "Remember what happened in the office this morning?"

"What happened in the office this morning?" I look between each of them for an explanation.

She waves it off. "He got a little agitated—"

"He damn near assaulted her too!" Watkins interrupts.

"He didn't lay a finger on me!" she counters.

The older man puts up his hands in surrender. "I'm just saying, we picked him up for assaulting a woman. Last I checked, you're a woman."

"Last I checked, I was still a cop too," she fires back.

He shakes his head but doesn't say anything else. Harkness crosses her arms and stares through the glass.

The room goes quiet. The man in the interview room rocks in his chair, his lips moving but no sound coming from them—at least, nothing that we can hear through the speakers.

"So what's the next move, boss?" Lawson asks.

The question hangs for another moment before she says, "I'm going back in. *Alone.*"

"Jen," Watkins starts, but Harkness cuts him off.

"*Walt.*" Her eyes challenge him.

He sighs heavy. Angry. Then says, "Lawson, I want you standing right outside that door in case anything happens. And Harkness, use your head."

"Always do." She steps to the door and exits with Lawson right behind her.

In the moment before she enters the interview room, Watkins mutters to himself, "Damn, she's frustrating sometimes."

"Hello again." Through the glass, I see Harkness retake her seat.

The man looks up at her and stops rocking when she returns to the interview room.

"Just me now," she says.

"I'm not dumb." He looks through the glass, almost directly at me, as if he can see me. "I know they're still watching."

"Just forget about them," she says. "Focus on me. Do you mind if I ask you your name?"

The rocking returns.

"He's not going to tell her anything," Watkins says.

Chapter Three

"Right now we're calling you John Doe and that just seems so impersonal. Especially since you're right here and we can ask. It's the first connection we can make to finding your daughter. I want to help save her for you."

A moment passes, but the man finally says, "Donald Douglas."

"That's your name?"

He nods.

Even though I can only see the back of her head, I can tell she's smiling her kindest smile at him.

"Let's get searching on—" Watkins turns to talk to Lawson before remembering he sent him into the hallway. Grumbling, he gets up and hurries out of the room.

"Okay Donald, let me ask you about Joanie," Harkness says. "Your daughter?"

Slightly, he shakes his head, but Harkness ignores it.

"How old is she?"

"She's—well, it's not 19—I don't..." His voice wavers, then trails off.

"I know you're a bit confused about what year it is, but let's focus on the last time you saw her. Is she a teenager? Adult? Still a child?"

"Uh—she's a, uh, teenager."

"Okay," she says softly. "When was the last time you saw her?"

"This morning—or yesterday morning, or whatever time it is." He covers his face with his hand. "It all blends together."

"Was it before you left for work?"

"Yeah. She was going to work herself, too."

"Where does she work?"

"She does billing for a printing company. City Print Professionals."

"And where do you work?"

"Well, I'm finishing up at Ellsworth Energy. Processing what we have left from the mines, but I've been told I'm going to be laid off by the end of the year."

Harkness changes tactics. "Do you happen to know your daughter's phone number so we can try to track her calls?"

Donald's eyes narrow. "It's the same as mine. The house number."

"Oh okay. What's the number?" she asks, pen poised and ready. "Again, we just want to get a copy of the phone records to see if there's any suspicious activity. I know you're scared about what might happen to her, but I assure you, the more we know the better."

He nods and recites his number.

"Thank you for that."

Watkins comes back in the observation room with a laptop propped in one hand. He plops back in his seat and types away on the keyboard. "No prior arrest for Mr. Douglas. At least, none since 2005 when the records were digitized."

Of course not, if he's from 1969, I think to myself. *We might be rewriting history with every interaction with this man.*

"What kind of relationship do you have with your daughter?" Harkness asks.

"What do you mean 'what kind of relationship'? She's my daughter. I'd do anything for her."

"So she'd have no reason to run away?"

"No, of course not."

"No recent arguments or fights?"

"Well, we did get into it pretty badly recently."

"Oh?" she asks. "About what?"

"She said she wanted to get a tattoo of some bird or something."

"A tattoo?"

"Yes, she wanted to permanently mark up her body like some hoodlum," Donald says. "And she claims it was in honor of her mother who died several years ago."

Watkins leans over to the transcriber. "Hoodlum?"

"How bad was this fight?" Harkness asks.

Staring off, he nods slowly. "Pretty bad. She refused to talk to me for a whole day. We never really apologized, just went on as if we hadn't fought about it."

"Do you think she would run away because of it?"

"No!" he barks. "I told you before, I saw pictures!"

Watkins gets to his feet and rushes to the door. "Lawson, you ready?"

"Wait!" I call to him. "She's getting him to settle down."

"Yes, that's right," she says. "You did say that. From the man with the leather mask?"

"Yeah, it was him."

"Can you tell me more about how he looked?"

Donald's brow furrows as he thinks it over. "Uh…long coat. Boots. Dark clothing under the coat. He had a bit of a limp or something. He didn't walk quite right. But he was quick."

My heart begins to race.

"Quick how?" she asks quietly.

"He was able to overpower my teenaged daughter." His voice grows louder, angrier. Jaw clenching, face turning red. "He followed her, chased her down, and tied her up! God only knows what else he—"

Tears stop Donald from continuing. He covers his mouth with one hand and wipes his eyes with the other in an effort to hide his anguish.

Harkness rises to her feet. "I promise, we'll do everything we can to find your daughter. If you remember anything else that might be helpful, please let us know."

I get to my feet and follow Watkins out to the hallway to meet her.

"It's obvious what happened," Watkins says once Harkness shuts the door behind her. "He went off his meds, had a fight with his daughter, roughed her up, and his demented mind twisted the story to create this masked guy."

"They were fighting about a *tattoo*?" Lawson asks. "That seems…insignificant."

"Everyone's different, but if he really thinks it's 1969, then getting a tattoo back then—especially a woman—was a big deal." Harkness addresses Watkins. "And let me remind you, Detective, that your theory is currently all speculation. If you believe that's what really happened, find me the evidence to prove it."

"Find the daughter?" He takes a folder from Harkness.

"Bingo," she says. "Let me know what you find."

With a huff, he turns and walks off.

Unfazed, Harkness continues to dole out orders. "Officer Lawson, please escort Mr. Douglas back to his holding cell until he can officially be moved to the psychiatric center. His daughter might be missing, but he still assaulted the woman in the park. Perhaps those pending charges can be used as leverage once he's on medication."

Reaching for his handcuffs at his waist, Lawson steps into the interview room.

With everyone else gone, Harkness addresses me. "And you." She reaches for my arm and pulls me off to the side for when Lawson and Douglas pass by. "I'd like to debrief with you."

"Somewhere private?" I ask.

"It won't take long. Right here should be fine. What do you think? Does Watkins's theory have any merit?"

"If I didn't know better, then sure. But Donald Douglas described the Gatekeeper to a T. He's involved. I just need to figure out how."

"What do you know about this guy?"

"His real name is Arlus Cain."

Her brow furrows. "Cain…I know that name."

"CEO of River Valley Holdings. Apparently, also my little brother."

Shaking her head, she says, "Wait. Your *little* brother?"

Chapter Three

"Yep." I nod.

"How is that possible?"

"Not quite sure myself, but we have some theories."

"So what do you know about Arlus? Is he a sex offender or something? Why would he want to take a teenaged girl? And does he even have the power to move someone through time like Douglas claims? I can't believe I'm seriously asking that question."

"I'm not sure," I admit. "He's powerful, that's for sure. And I don't think he has any sort of sexual thing for Douglas's daughter. It's probably more—"

The interview room door opens and Officer Lawson leads Donald Douglas out into the hallway. Harkness and I both turn to them and I further step out of the way, but when Douglas lays eyes on me, his face turns to pure venom.

Suddenly becoming uncooperative, he lunges at me. Lawson tugs at his arm from behind and Harkness tries to wedge her way between us in the cramped hallway.

"That's him!" Douglas shouts. "That's the one! I've found him! It's over!"

"Hey, that's enough!" Harkness shouts, likely to draw the attention of her colleagues in the office around the corner.

Lawson loses his grip and Douglas charges at me. Luckily, two other officers from down the hall are already right on top of us. Both of them tackle him down to the floor. I stand, frozen where I am, wondering what my connection to this is. He didn't mention a single thing about me in the interview. Only the Gatekeeper and his daughter. Why the sudden rage?

The officers get Donald back on his feet and try to pull him away, but he still manages to launch a spitball right in my face before he's dragged away down the hall.

Chapter Four

ASH

"Can you fast track it, please?" Harkness asks into the phone. "His name is Donald Douglas. We just identified him. No, it's not—we just need—yeah, I'll hold." Covering the receiver, she says to me, "Judges and their power trips."

Sitting in the chair beside her desk, I sip my first cup of coffee of the day. We rushed out so quickly this morning that I didn't have time to make a cup. It's only marginally helping. How do you recover from being spit on? Despite my absent memory, I can say confidently that this was certainly not the warmest good morning greeting I've ever received.

"Hi, Judge Hanson?" she suddenly says excitedly into the phone. "It's Detective Jenna Harkness with the Ellsworth Police Department. Yeah, hi. Listen, I just submitted a request for inmate Donald Douglas to be transferred to Wardle Psychiatric Center— No, he hasn't been formally charged with anything yet, but— No, he hasn't consented…. Truthfully, I don't believe he'd agree to go so this would be an emergency transfer request….

Chapter Four

Well, as I stated in my report, he was arrested for assaulting a woman in a park, he refuses to speak to men, and he spit on one of my witnesses."

Leaning on her desk, she rubs her forehead and closes her eyes as she listens. "Sir, with all due respect, I disagree. He believes it's still 1969. If that's not an example of a mental illness, then I don't know what else I can do to convince you." She listens again for a minute and then sighs heavily. "No, I understand. Thank you anyway."

Slamming the phone back in its cradle, she presses her palms against her forehead.

"Bad news?" I ask.

Another heavy sigh. "He won't approve a transfer. Says Douglas either has to agree to go voluntarily or a doctor would have to make the recommendation."

"The assaults didn't make a difference?"

"Doesn't prove that he's mentally unfit." Her eyes venture down toward my chin, where Donald Douglas's loogie landed earlier. "Sorry about before."

"It's not your fault. So what does that mean now? What are you going to do with Donald Douglas while we sort through all this?"

"It means he's going to stay in our jail until we try him for something. We have twenty-four hours." Glancing up at the clock, she adds, "Actually, more like twenty hours since he was picked up early this morning."

"How do we get started?"

"The woman he scared this morning is fine. Officer Lawson just got in touch with her and she said she's not going to press charges, which means that in theory we could let Douglas go."

"But you're not going to do that."

"Not with the story he told us about his daughter. Detective Watkins has a point: Douglas *could* be the one who kidnapped her, which means we need to take precautions."

"But he didn't kidnap his daughter. He described the Gate-keeper perfectly. So we know my brother is involved."

She shakes her head. "We don't know that for sure. All we know is what Douglas told me in the interview, which still needs to be verified. Right now, I have Watkins following the lead that Donald Douglas is responsible, but I don't have high hopes for that. You and I will be looking into the possibility that it's this Gatekeeper guy. But first thing's first: I need you to tell me everything you know about him so we can come up with a better list of suspects."

Leaning forward, I rest my arms against my knees and lower my voice so only Harkness can hear me. The open office makes me nervous about talking so freely about this. "Uh, well, like I said, his real name is, uh, Arlus Cain."

Harkness writes on a blank piece of notebook paper as I talk.

"Um, he started River Valley Holdings…a long time ago," I continue. "I don't remember specifically, but I know he grew it from the ground up. What else? Uh…oh, he hates me for some reason."

"You mentioned that. Does it have anything to do with your relation? Or is this Heat related?"

I shrug. "I don't know. He claims I know what I did, but with my head I don't remember. So it must be from when we were younger."

She nods once in acknowledgment. "And you don't remember anything from back then?"

"Well, *I* don't remember, no. But I do know some stuff that happened back then that has had effects into today."

"Like what?"

"I already told you that technically he's my little brother. And I heard from my old girlfriend that he survived the coal mine explosion in 1969."

"The same year Douglas thinks it is now."

"Yeah. Do you think it's significant?"

"I don't think it's *insignificant*," she says. "But we'll get back to that. Anything else? When was the last time you had contact with him?"

"Let's use the word 'contact' loosely here. I haven't *really* had a conversation with him. Every time I've seen him, it's usually been between Heat and the Gatekeeper—and we're kicking each other's asses."

She gives me a look.

"Okay, he was usually kicking *my* ass," I admit. "Which is why we're in this predicament to begin with. We're not still worrying about Dust Storm or Black Magnet, are we? I did just fine on my own with them."

Her head perks up. "Black Magnet? There was another bad super?"

"Forget about him. It's been taken care of. Anyway, the last time I saw the Gatekeeper was when I kicked him off the top of the Fenty Building."

Another look, this time confusion.

"Obviously he survived," I add. "I didn't check to see what happened to him at the time because ESTR was on fire. But, that's basically all I know about him."

"Okay," she says as she exhales. "That got a little too far-fetched for my liking, so I'm going to go off of what I *do* know. It sounds like you and Arlus have history that's fueling this feud between you two and instead of confronting each other like mature adults, he's involving other people."

"He's gotta protect his name," I say. "Arlus Cain is a respected businessman. If it comes out that he started the fire storm that set the city ablaze, then he's going to lose a few clients."

"Yes, I get that. And on some level, I guess I get the masks. What I don't understand is why he hasn't confronted you privately like a rational person. If he really did start River Valley from scratch, then he's not a stupid man. Actually, a businessman like that would probably welcome the idea of a meeting, even if it's confrontational. So why does he want to kill you instead of just hash it out in an intense conversation?"

"Maybe he's not a rational person?"

She shakes her head. "This weirdness with the supers didn't start until you—until Heat showed up. If you were really gone for fifty years, that means that Arlus has had fifty years to get over it. So obviously you did—or he *thinks* you did—something unforgivable that he'd still be mad about today. Something he'd want to *kill* you for."

Shrugging, I say, "I don't know what that is, though. I know I was in the coal mine when it exploded too. I wasn't supposed to be, but I ran in to save our parents. But Arlus is the only one from my family who walked out alive that day. I went *somewhere* and our parents…"

"Maybe seeing you stirred up the pain of losing his family all those years ago. Instead of being grateful that you're alive, he blames you for being in that mine when you shouldn't have been."

I shake my head. "No, the Gatekeeper first attacked before I even knew he existed. The fire storm hit when it was just me, Ra—" I bite my tongue in time to spare exposing Rachel and Perry. "Just me and a couple people I had met."

"Maybe somehow *he* knew you were back and that's why he started the fire storm."

"Maybe."

"Do you know if he was married?" she asks. "Does it have something to do with his wife or children?"

"He *was* married, but after the fire. And I don't *think* he was seeing anyone during the time of the fire, but I could be wrong. I wish I could remember."

Collecting her papers together, Harkness straightens them and lays them back down on her desk. "I know, but you're going to need to remember. Doesn't sound like your brother is going to tell you why he's mad so we need to figure it out before he can hurt anymore people."

"I've been trying to remember, but I—"

"Try harder," she says firmly. "This isn't just about you anymore. This is about making sure that no one else gets hurt because of some stupid childhood grudge. People are *dying*, Ash. We need to resolve this immediately."

The death of my parents doesn't seem all that stupid to me, but I let it slide. Harkness is right. It's up to me to pull together what I can to figure out why Arlus hates me, even after so many years when I was presumed to be dead.

Perry mentioned he was working on something that might be able to help me recover some of my lost memories. If that doesn't work, maybe Rachel can help me scour old newspaper articles from the time of the fire to piece it together. And there's always Linda. She could possibly have some old photos from when we were younger that might stir up even more of my memories. But I don't want to burden her too much. Seems like she's found a way to move past everything that happened all those years ago. When I visited her, that was closure for her. Best not to reopen old wounds.

"I'll come up with something," I tell Harkness.

"Good." She smiles reassuringly. "In the meantime, I'll put together a team to figure out Arlus's whereabouts. I'll need to come up with a reason why we're looking into him. Don't worry, I won't tell them about your connection to him."

"You could tell them that Heat tipped you off," I offer.

She shakes her head. "That's murky water. Unfortunately, Heat's testimony is essentially useless."

"Why?"

"He wears a mask. Nobody knows for sure whether it's the same person underneath, which means naming him as a witness would be questionable in a trial."

"So I'm really not much help, am I?"

Harkness gives me a sad look. "I want to get him too. But

I want to do it the right way so that he's *legally* required to stay behind bars. That's going to take some work."

"Yeah, I guess that makes sense."

"That's not to say that Heat can't assist with the investigation—off the record," she says. "Like I said on the phone, you have unique expertise in this area."

I smirk. "You already know I wouldn't just sit on the sidelines anyway."

"Oh no, I'm fully aware of that. And I don't even want to think about how we're going to keep this Gatekeeper guy *physically* behind bars."

"Actually, I might have someone who can help with that."

"Another friend?" she asks.

"Maybe. But I want to hold off on promising anything until I talk to hi—them."

She rolls her eyes at my clumsy concealment. "Whatever. That's good, though. But I've still got my work cut out for me. We're going to need to put together a good case if it really is the Gatekeeper—and then prove that Arlus Cain is really the man behind it all. Otherwise, it's not going to hold up in court."

"I saw him as the Gatekeeper. He took off his mask and used his powers in front of me. Plus, he even admitted it."

Again, she shakes her head. This time before I even finish talking. "Not if it was Heat who saw him as the Gatekeeper. And if it was Heat who heard Arlus say that he's the Gatekeeper, we're back at square one. Heat's testimony doesn't mean anything. Not with the anonymity."

Rolling my head back in frustration, I stare up at the fluorescent lights on the ceiling. How does the Gatekeeper keep evading punishment like this? Except, Heat wasn't alone when the Gatekeeper revealed himself to be Arlus Cain. But that would mean involving my friends in a criminal case that could also put a target on their backs if we don't have a prison equipped to contain Arlus. Even if we do, we already know Arlus gave Vernon his powers that made him Black Magnet. And he probably did the same with Dust Storm too. He's not above hiring a hitman—or rather, *creating* one—to take out the people who stand in his way.

"I know some people who heard and saw the same thing I did—or Heat did—about Arlus and the Gatekeeper, but I'll need to talk to them first," I tell her. "They might not agree to help for their own protection."

"Understandable," she says. "But any extra testimony will only help our case. And if we're going to pull this off, it needs to be rock solid."

Chapter Five
Detective Harkness

ot an update for you." Walter Watkins approaches Harkness's desk with his eyes on the manila folder in his hand.

"You found some stuff on Donald Douglas?" she asks, hopeful.

"Well, I'm not sure it's *our* Donald Douglas," he says. "I called the DMV and they found a license, but it's not—"

"Just tell me."

"This guy must be thorough with this hoax, because the only Donald Douglas they had on file was issued a license in 1966. Date of birth on that license was February 20, 1918, so definitely not our guy."

"Any death record?" she asks. "That was over a hundred years ago, so the likelihood of him still being alive is slim."

He shakes his head. "No death record and after 1966, the license was never renewed."

"Interesting," she murmurs. That could explain the time

jump. "Of course, he could've just moved out of state, or even the country."

"True, but the man we have in custody is in his forties or fifties," Watkins says. "Not his early 100s."

"Right. Yeah."

"What have you found?" he asks.

"Stuff from the same general time period." She scrolls through the page on her computer. "In our database, there's an arrest report for a Donald Douglas from 1950."

Watkins sits on the edge of her desk and folds his arms, the manila folder peeking out near his opposite side. "What were the charges?"

"Assault. Bar fight."

"Similar to what our guy is in for," he notes. "Maybe it's his father and the whole family has anger issues. Could be why there's no license issued to Donald Douglas after 1966."

"But there are no other arrests after 1950," she says. "And, get this, the only record for a Joanie Douglas I could find is a birth announcement from 1951."

Watkins pinches the bridge of his nose. "Okay, this man is seriously off his rocker. That would be his…sister, right?"

She shakes her head. "I don't think that's the case, honestly. Let's roll with the idea that the Donald Douglas we have is telling the truth and he thinks it's 1969."

He rolls his eyes, but doesn't say anything else.

"If he was born in 1918, like you found, that would make him fifty-one in 1969, right?"

Her partner does the math in his head and nods. "Right."

"And if Joanie was *born* in 1951 and Douglas is saying it's 1969, that means that she's eighteen."

"Your point?" he asks, frustrated.

"My point is, Douglas is in his fifties and he said his daughter is a teenager. The math is adding up."

"Except for the fact that 1969 was *fifty* years ago!" His

voice rings across the office.

Detective Harkness bites her tongue. With what she's found—and what she's witnessed with the Dust Storm case—she believes Donald Douglas is telling the truth, which means there's a girl out there who needs help.

"What did you find on Joanie Douglas?" she asks in a much quieter voice.

He clears his throat, unfolds his arms, and opens the folder to the correct printout. "Uh, no missing persons reports. I called all the high schools in the city and no one's seen anyone fitting her description."

"Donald said she worked at City Print Professionals," she says. "Didn't sound like she was in high school anymore."

"Well, that's the problem. City Print Professionals closed in 1986."

Harkness leans back in her chair and looks up to the ceiling, frustrated that all the leads for Joanie are dead-ends.

"But I called around to other area printing companies and asked if they have anyone employed fitting her description," he says. "I'm still waiting on a few places to call me back, but…" He shakes his head.

She sighs heavily. "Okay. Thank you. Uh, why don't you see if you can call around to more judges to see if you can get someone to approve moving Douglas to Wardle. If he does need to go on meds, we need to get him straightened out as soon as possible. His daughter's life might depend on it."

Doubt lingers in Watkins's eyes, but he doesn't voice it. Simply nods and returns to his desk.

Back on her computer, Harkness reads through the rest of Joanie Douglas's birth announcement. Mary and Donald Douglas are listed as the parents. It's the first time Harkness has seen or heard mention of Joanie's mother.

Pulling up another tab, she searches for Mary Douglas and finds an obituary from 1956. Cause of death: heart attack.

Chapter Five

Survivors: her husband, Douglas, and her five-year-old daughter, Joanie.

The premature death of Mary made Donald a single parent. Harkness knows the dates of the events are significant so she plays a little game of make-believe to try to make sense of them. If Donald Douglas had a drinking problem when he was younger, that seemed to stop after the birth of Joanie. At least, that's what would make sense. But not all alcohol-related incidents were reported back then and the police filing system has changed a lot since then with digitalization. Other arrest reports could've gotten lost in the shuffle.

Still, Harkness can't believe that a single father would want to hurt his own daughter. Especially not when she's already grown up with her own job. It doesn't make sense.

Going back to the birth announcement, Harkness finishes reading through it and notes that the place of employment for Donald says Ellsworth Energy. The large coal manufacturer that used to dominate Ellsworth's economy. The same place that harvested the coal from the mines in the mountains where Arlus and Ash's parents worked.

Smiling, Harkness stares at her computer screen and mutters, "Looks like I just found the connection."

———

HARKNESS'S FIST RAPS against the tall mahogany door behind the white sandstone pillars holding up the roof overhanging from the second story. Above her hangs a black lantern chandelier, which likely is more for decoration than illumination.

No answer, so she tries again. There's no doorbell—not even a door knocker. Clearly, Arlus Cain does not welcome uninvited guests. Detective Harkness herself hasn't ever been up to the estates on the backside of the mountain west of the city. The same mountain the coal mines run through, but on the city's side of the mountain. From here, the views are the rest of the mountain range, which likely boasts a beautiful sunset. It's a way to be close to the city without having to look at it. Just what she'd expect from someone like Arlus Cain.

Stepping to the side, Harkness peers through the large window. Sheer curtains are pulled closed, but there's enough light from other windows in the house that she can see inside. The furniture looks plush and new. Everything seems tidy and well-kept. Certainly not like it's been lived in, although it is homey—

"Can I help you?"

Whirling around, Harkness reaches for her gun. Standing just off the large front porch is a man in coveralls, wiping his hands in a rag. Sweat dribbles down his face from his dark hair to his pointed chin. At the other end of the driveway, she spots an ATV equipped with a wagon and gardening tools. That explains how the lawn has been mowed and the gardens remain pristine.

"Oh, yes." She tries to regain her composure and descends the stairs to greet him. "I'm Detective Harkness, Ellsworth Police Department. I'm looking for Arlus Cain, do you know if he's home?"

The man shakes his head. "He hasn't been home in a while, far as I can tell."

"Do you know when he might be back?"

He shrugs. "Hard to say. It's not unusual for him to head off on a trip to Maui or Europe or whatever his flavor of the week is. If you ask me, he's worked hard enough, he deserves to take some vacation time now that he's up there in years."

"So you don't have any idea where he might've gone?"

"No, ma'am."

Harkness grumbles. "And you are?"

"Miles Leach." He extends his grubby hand. "I'm Mr. Cain's personal maintenance man."

She shakes his hand, then asks, "What exactly do you maintain?"

Chapter Five

"Grounds, mostly," he says. "But I make sure none of the pipes are bursting inside during the winter months and I service the HVAC systems inside all year. I'm the handyman. Odds and ends, stuff like that."

Harkness points back to the front door. "Could you let me inside?"

Miles looks put-off. "Why would you want to go inside?"

"To make sure he's not passed out somewhere," she lies.

"I've been in and out every so often this past week," he says. "I would've seen something."

"And you've checked the whole house?"

He clears his throat and looks down at his feet. Despite the fact that he towers over her, he cowers to her questions. "Well, no…"

"So you don't really know if he's all right, do you?"

"I guess not. But I don't think—Mr. Cain likes his privacy. I could be out of a job if he's in there and I let you in and—"

Harkness puts up a hand to stop him. "Okay, okay. But I got a call from someone who's concerned about him." She decides to leave out the part that that someone is Ash and his concern is that Arlus is going to kill more people. "If you prevent me from getting in and potentially saving him, then you may be facing criminal charges."

Miles's eyes open wide in shock.

"Suddenly the possibility of getting fired doesn't seem so bad, does it?"

"No." He steps up to the porch and pulls out his keys. "I'll let you in. Just…take off your shoes before you step on the carpet."

When the door is open, Harkness steps in first and kicks off her shoes by the doormat. She looks around at the large room with tall ceilings and even more decorative support beams. To the left, a curved staircase leads up to the second floor, with a banister allowing those above to look down on the front room. The sheer curtains on all the windows are drawn, casting the house into dimmed lighting. The air is stuffy. No hint of an open window anywhere.

"Do you mind if I look around?" she asks Miles as she takes a step onto the white carpet.

"Uh, yeah. That's fine, I guess."

To the right, a cased opening leads into a formal dining room with a long glass table. Just off of that is a large kitchen with marble countertops and hardwood floors.

"Uh, Mr. Cain doesn't usually spend too much time in the kitchen," Miles says nervously from behind her.

"I just need to be thorough." She opens the fridge and looks at the contents. Several bottles of water, butter, condiments. No milk or eggs, suggesting he either isn't coming back anytime soon or hasn't been home in a while. "Is his bedroom upstairs?"

"I don't know if I should let you—"

"What's the point of coming in here if we're not even going to check the whole house?"

He nods and leads her back out to the main room.

At the top of the stairs, a large antique china cabinet catches Harkness's eye. It's nothing like the rest of the furniture, being that it's old and filled with personal pictures. She bends to look at them all, instantly recognizing a younger Ash smiling with his arm around another boy, likely Arlus.

On the next shelf up sits a picture of two straight-lipped adults on what appears to be their wedding day. The woman is wearing a lacy white gown and the man is in a traditional black suit. Beside that sits a book with handwritten entries:

The Martin Family – Deepest sympathies
Jessica and Mike – Our condolences
Terry Lewis – Thinking of you

It's the guestbook from his parents' funeral.

"Miles, I think you have a point," Harkness says suddenly.

Chapter Five

"What's that?"

"I think it would be best if you checked on Mr. Cain's bedroom to make sure nothing is wrong. It'd be better than a stranger."

"Oh. Okay." He starts off down the hall.

"Don't be hasty. Make sure to check every room up here, just in case."

"Yes, ma'am, I will."

She waits for him to disappear around the corner before opening the china cabinet and pulling out the guestbook. Starting at the beginning, she scans each entry as quick as she can. Finally, three pages in she sees what she's looking for. Scrawled at the bottom of the page reads:

Donald Douglas – Your parents were wonderful friends. Sorry to have lost them. Call me if you ever need anything.

So Donald Douglas and the Cains were friends. And his entry in the guestbook was very clearly directed at Arlus since he was the only known survivor. Perhaps Arlus kept tabs on Douglas and knew that he was a single father with a teenaged daughter. Someone close in age to Arlus and who might've even been friends with him.

Makes for plenty of opportunity to kidnap her as a bribe.

———

"HONESTLY, I'M NOT all that surprised that a police officer is looking into Arlus," Carolyn Skitter says as she takes a seat in her living room with a cup of tea in her hands. She adjusts the gold chain around her neck, tucking it safely back in her enhanced cleavage.

Arlus's ex-wife lives just outside downtown in an old brick Victorian. Not shy about her own money, the small front garden overflows with beautiful flowers of all colors while the bright green grass is carefully and meticulously trimmed along the edges of the sidewalk. Not a single speck of chipping paint can be seen on the old house.

Inside, hardwood floors stretch back to the white kitchen, which is illuminated brightly, inviting visitors to sit and chat in the assortment of plush seating options on the first floor. While Arlus's house was certainly beautiful, Carolyn's is much more inviting.

"Why would you say that?" Harkness asks as she takes a seat.

"Oh, he was always impressed with his own status," she says with a wave of her hand, as if what she's saying is common knowledge. Her long painted fingernails draw attention to the several rings on her fingers. "Never wanted to be known as the orphan boy. Instead he wanted to be known as the boss."

"There's nothing inherently wrong with that."

"Not the way Arly used to act," she says. "Always had to be the best, the richest, the most interesting. He didn't used to be so conceited. No, he was sweet, even a little shy when we were younger."

"And now he's not?"

"Honey, he's the CEO of a major investment company," she says with a laugh. "He can't be nice in that world!"

"Surely he was nice on some level, if you married him."

"Oh, so you're here for the story, aren't you, dear?"

"I suppose I am," Harkness says with a shrug. She feels especially *simple* in the presence of Carolyn and her big personality.

"Arly and I dated a bit in high school," she says. "Gosh, this is going back about fifty years. Oh my, we're getting up there." She sets her tea cup down on the small table beside her and continues, "In hindsight, I suppose we only got married because all of our friends were. And, if I'm being honest, I think Arly just didn't want to be alone anymore. You heard what happened to his family, right?"

Harkness nods. "Yes, it's very sad."

"It was terrible. He was heartbroken. His spirit was crushed. To tell you the truth, dear, I don't think he was ever the same after that. How could you be? In one day, he lost his entire family, while *he* was one of the people who were trying to save them!"

The detective opens her mouth to reply, but Carolyn talks over her.

"After that he quit the fire department, dropped out of school, became almost like a recluse for a couple months," she says. "And he won't ever admit to this because he's 'the man,' but it was *me* who suggested we get married. I thought it'd liven him up and at the time, it seemed right.

"My mother thought I was crazy marrying a deadbeat like he was at the time, but before our wedding he went back to school for business, started working again, and pulled himself up to be a responsible person, just like he was before. But he was different."

"Different how?"

"He just seemed broken. And as his new wife, I didn't know what I was doing wrong. Shouldn't I have made him happy? I know he lost his family, but look at everything he had gained since then." She shakes her head and looks out the front window. "I know pain like that never really goes away, but I thought I could offer him a proper distraction. And FYI, sweetheart—since I don't see a ring on your finger—that's not a good foundation for a successful marriage, let me tell you that."

"No, of course not."

"But I was a fool then," she goes on. "I got pregnant pretty early on. Early 70s, I think. Now *that* changed Arly's attitude. Suddenly I could see glimpses of the man I knew when we were teenagers. When Amy came, she was his world…until things got difficult."

Harkness's eyebrows go up. "Difficult?"

"Oh, he never beat us or anything like that, but he went back to that reclusive behavior again," Carolyn explains. "Never wanted to do things as a family. Barely held Amy as she got older and needed more attention. By then, I wasn't the pushover little girl anymore. No dear, I was getting fed up with the way things were. We argued a lot. I'm sure Amy saw more than we should've let her see. But I stayed because of her. Because that's what wives did back then. They stuck it out and made it work."

She chuckles.

"Obviously, I think differently now, although my husband and I have been married for almost as long as I was married to Arlus."

"How long was that?" Harkness asks.

"Well, we married in 1970." She stares up at the opposite wall with narrowed eyes, thinking. "Amy passed away in 1991, but we didn't officially divorce until three years later. So what is that? About twenty-four years? Yeah, that sounds right. Hank and I just celebrated twenty-three years together and, sweetheart, let me tell you, it's like night and day between the two marriages."

Smiling politely, Harkness says, "I bet. But, if you don't mind, can we backtrack and talk about how Arlus was around the time of your daughter's passing?"

Carolyn stares at her and swallows hard. "Yes, dear," she says softly. "Arlus and Amy…didn't have a good relationship, toward the end. How could they when he refused to have anything to do with her? But he loved her, in his own way. But although her death made me unbelievably heartbroken, Arlus had already been through pain like that. And worse. No, when our Amy passed, he became angry."

"Angry? At who?"

"Everyone. Everything. It didn't matter. That's why it took three years for us to officially divorce. I was afraid of what he would do to me if I didn't agree to stay."

"Agree to stay? Did you try leaving him before?"

"Yes, a few months after Amy passed. He was…" She clutches

at her chest. "He was livid when I served him with divorce papers. Terrifying. So I agreed to stay to save my own life. I've never been through something so…" She breathes in a deep breath with her eyes closed. "After three years, things weren't any better, as you can probably imagine. At that point, I had secured a spot at a safe house and served him again. I haven't seen him since our divorce was final and, to be honest, I'm happy with that."

Harkness sits and waits for Carolyn to collect herself before asking, "Do you remember what Arlus's relationship was like with his brother back then?"

"His brother?" she asks. "What was his name? Uh…Abel?"

"Ash."

"Oh," she forces a smile. "My mistake. Cain and Abel has always popped into my mind with that last name. Even when it was mine!" She chuckles, regaining parts of her previous carefree persona. "It's hard for me to remember since it was so long ago, but I don't believe there was anything remarkable about it. They were brothers. They bickered. They fought. But from what I remember, they seemed to care for each other."

"But Arlus never said anything about Ash?"

"He never talked about any of his family after the fire," she says. "It was too painful for him, as you can imagine. Why do you ask? What kind of trouble is Arlus in?"

"Well, he hasn't been seen in several weeks," Harkness says. "And several of his…contacts have been involved in some serious crimes, so we just wanted to check in with him. His absence is…suspicious."

"I see. Have you checked his office? Ever since he started River Valley, he has been a slave to it. It was all I could do to even get ten percent of that, since it was started during our marriage."

Harkness nods. "Yes, I checked the office. They didn't seem too concerned. Said he often disappears unannounced for weeks on end to travel."

Carolyn scoffs. "See what I'm telling you about status? He

needs everyone to know that he can pop off on vacation whenever the whim arises. But, you know, good for him. He's certainly given up everything for that."

Again, Detective Harkness smiles politely as she rises to her feet. "Well, thank you for talking with me."

"Oh, no, dear, it was a pleasant visit—even if we were discussing my ex-husband," she says, following her guest to the door. "I do hope I was helpful in some way."

"You certainly helped me better understand Arlus Cain." Which is about all she did…

"Yes, well, unfortunately Arlus went through *serious* trauma when he was young and it has had effects on his entire life. The death of his family significantly scarred him. I don't believe he's ever truly moved passed it."

Chapter Six

ASH

In the real world, Heat is useless." Flopping back on the couch, I stare up at the ceiling in Perry's living room. My eyes follow the slow-spinning ceiling fan, causing ancient cobwebs in the corner of the popcorn ceiling to sway.

"What the hell did I ask?" Perry chuckles from his seat in the kitchen. He's sitting at the counter eating a sandwich and scrolling through his phone. On my way in, all he said was, "Hey," and that prompted my declaration about Heat.

Sitting up, I ask, "You know how you dropped me off at the police station this morning?"

"You mean the reason we dashed out of here in a mad rush on my morning off? Yeah, it's ringing a bell."

Ignoring Perry's quip, I go on, "The police picked up a man at Riverside Park for assaulting a woman early this morning."

"And why is that your concern?" He takes a bite and then asks with a mouthful, "Is the woman okay?"

"Yeah, I guess she's fine. But the guy they picked up seemed odd to Detective Harkness."

"Odd?" he asks between chews.

"Off his rocker. Looney. Nutsy. Weird. Insane." With each description, I make an equally strange face.

"Okay, I get it."

I smile. "No, but seriously he was very agitated and I guess at one point he told an officer that it was 1969."

Perry's eyebrows go up. "Your 1969?"

"And here I was thinking that it was *everyone's* 1969."

"You know what I mean!"

"Yes, my 1969. Anyway, he started talking about a man in a leather mask who took his daughter and that the man was going to hurt her if he didn't find them. That's why Harkness called me in."

"Because she knows you're from the 60s?"

"Right. So she went in and questioned him and he described the Gatekeeper perfectly, which means—"

"He's getting ready to make his move," Perry finishes.

"Exactly. And since he used Vernon—and very likely Dr. Isaacs, too—to try to get to me before, I'm suspecting that this crazy man down at the police station is the next innocent victim who has involuntarily signed up to be my next hitman."

My friend doesn't seem as convinced. "I don't know. I mean, Vernon was probably chosen because of his connection to us."

I shake my head. "No, Arlus had Vernon wrapped around his finger for years because of what happened with Arlus's daughter."

My niece.

Amy.

"Refresh my memory with that again," he says.

"Vernon accidentally killed Arlus's daughter in a bad car crash and as repayment, Vernon needed to work for Arlus and do whatever he told him to do."

"Like work at River Valley Holdings and become the account rep for ESTR," Perry adds.

"Which sat right outside the gate for the trail that leads up to the old coal mine I woke up in," I finish. "It wasn't a coincidence that Vernon was there."

"Okay, so why wouldn't Arlus put all the people who owed him favors in that building?" he asks. "That would guarantee that the right person would find you when you woke up. It seems like an awfully big risk for Arlus to take if he wanted you to get in touch with one of his lackeys. And not just that, not everyone at ESTR worked for Arlus in that way. I, for one, know that *I* don't owe Arlus anything. And I very much doubt that Rachel does. It seems very coincidental that Vernon—who was already friends with us before you showed up—was one of the first people to stumble on you right after you got out of the cave."

"The only thing that I can come up with is that Arlus knew I was on my way. And whether it was Vernon, you, Rachel, or anyone else, Arlus would've made sure that one of his men—in this case, Vernon—showed up and got close to me so Arlus could keep an eye on me. And, if you remember, *Rachel* is the one who found me. She called you and then *suddenly* Vernon showed up shortly after. That wasn't the coincidence we thought it was."

"Let's backtrack here a bit. You think Arlus knew you were going to crawl out of the cave after fifty years?"

I shrug. "I don't know. But you and Rachel both said that I probably wasn't actually in that cave for fifty years, I was probably transported somewhere else. And yet somehow I didn't age. Maybe with Arlus's power, he was able to put me somewhere until he was ready for me. Somewhere that apparently warps time. Or maybe it was just an instantaneous thing. One second I was in 1969 and the next I was in 2019, but the split-second travel wiped my brain."

"But why would he push you off until later?"

"I don't know. That's what Harkness told me to figure out because of that crazy man from the park today—Donald Douglas. With him showing up and talking about someone who looks like the Gatekeeper tells us that my long-lost brother is involved. And he's come after me enough times for us to know that he wants to kill me and he'll drag down anyone and everyone until he does. We need to stop him."

"Maybe this Donald Douglas guy saw who the Gatekeeper really was, so if you show him a picture of Arlus, maybe he can confirm that it's him," Perry suggests.

I hold up my hand to stop him. "First of all, Harkness is going to need more. Douglas could lead her to pursue Arlus further, which she's already doing, by the way, but it's not going to be enough for her to arrest him. And second, Douglas described the Gatekeeper, not Arlus Cain. So he doesn't even know who the Gatekeeper really is."

"Oh. That makes sense." Perry takes the last bite of his sandwich and mumbles with a full mouth, "What's the background on this Donald Douglas guy? What's his connection to Arlus?"

"Still working on that," I say. "Not sure. Maybe he was a friend or a neighbor or something back then. I don't remember him, but that doesn't mean Arlus didn't know him then. Of course, it could also just be a random victim Arlus chose as leverage."

"Let's hope it's not that."

"Yeah. Either way, we need to find a way to point this in Arlus's direction and get him arrested." I lay back and bury my face in my hands. "Not that that's going to make a difference because no prison cell is equipped to contain him. He'll just open a portal and step out in Ethiopia or something."

"Ethiopia?"

Struggling to sit back up, I say, "It was the first country that popped into my head."

"Okay then," Perry says with an eye roll. "Does Harkness know where Arlus is?"

"She's putting together a team to try to find him and hopefully find some charges for them to bring him in on."

"All right, so this is where Heat *does* come in handy."

"You want me to just go out and find him? Perry, we've been searching since Vernon died. He's gone. Probably to Ethiopia!"

"Would you shut up about Ethiopia?" he says with a laugh. "And no, we haven't been searching as much as we should because,"—he lists each thing on his finger—"we were grieving Vernon's death, we had Dust Storm to deal with, and honestly, since the Gatekeeper hasn't caused any issues, he's kind of been put on the back burner because of *life*."

"Yeah, that's true."

"So this man popping up—Donald—it's a sign that things are about to get dicey. We need to be as prepared as we can be for whatever's coming. What does Harkness know about Arlus that we don't already know?"

"Nothing. She was asking *me* about him. He's not officially a criminal so he hasn't been on their radar because he's never needed to be. They're starting from scratch right now to figure out his motive and stuff. Well, she is. She needs to weigh all options because one of the other detectives thinks that Donald is the one who kidnapped his own daughter."

Perry lets out a long sigh. "The truth will come out one way or another. We've gotta do our part, though."

"I did spend the day looking into brother dearest," I say.

"How so?"

"See if there's anything that's incriminating in his past that Harkness can arrest him for—or at least question him about. Maybe then she can try to establish a connection with Crazy Don Douglas."

"What'd you find?"

"Nothing that can help with the case. At least, not directly."

"What do you mean?" Perry asks.

"Because he's a big businessman in Ellsworth, the *Gazette* did a long biography on him a few years ago in some 'Ellsworth Emerges' spotlight series that focused on the big names in the city. Anyway, Arlus was featured in one and I found out a lot of what he's been up to in the last fifty years—mostly professionally."

"And this helps how?"

"It gave me a clearer image of my brother in my own head because a lot of it seemed to click, subconsciously, with the person I knew back then. When Arlus was…twenty-one, I think?"

"He's only a year younger than you?"

I shrug. "I guess so. The article said he married in 1970 when he was twenty-two and Linda said I was twenty-two when I disappeared in 1969. And I'm just thinking about those visions I had about wrestling with that boy and I have to believe that that was Arlus and I was taking the older brother responsibilities of picking on him a little too seriously."

"Yeah, but just because your older brother was mean to you as a kid doesn't turn you into a manipulator who holds a grudge for fifty years."

"Maybe not, but it could've sowed the seeds for something bigger that happened when we were older."

"Maybe."

"Anyway, most of his story is kind of unremarkable. After he got married, he worked at a bank for twenty years before starting River Valley Holdings in the early 90s, which was around the time Amy was killed by Vernon and he went to work for Arlus and eventually the company grew."

"I take it they didn't mention Vernon killing Arlus's daughter in the article?"

"They didn't even mention that Arlus *had* a daughter," I say. "It's like she was erased from history."

"What about his wife? I don't remember Vernon ever talking about her."

"Didn't mention her either, really. Maybe she's dead."

"Or maybe she's very much alive," Perry says. "Look at your

old girlfriend. They're in their seventies, they're not necessarily on their deathbeds."

"Actually, hopefully she is alive and maybe they're even divorced or something," I go on. "Maybe Harkness will find *Ms.* Cain and she'll want to bash her ex-husband freely. If his ex has something incriminating on him, that would give Harkness reason to go after him."

"That's hoping he hasn't shut her up somehow."

"Like a bribe?"

"Or worse," he says. "I mean, look at Vernon."

"True."

"And none of this matters if Harkness can't even find him."

"Hopefully his ex-wife will be able to help with that."

"There's a lot of maybes in this."

I make a face. "I know. And Harkness says we need a solid case in order for it to hold up and get him convicted, which will be tricky because he has powers. It's not like we can turn him to glass like we did with Dust Storm."

"Maybe I can help with that," he says. "I'll try to come up with something that will dampen his powers. I already created a prototype for that once. I should be able to do it again. But in the meantime, I think you should call Detective Harkness. See where Heat can help find Arlus. If you can't, then you just need to trust her and her investigation to find him. Remember what happened last time you interfered?"

"Yeah, she decided to use me as an informant in future cases like this."

"*After* you got arrested!"

"It wasn't an arrest, only questioning!"

He lets out a heavy sigh. "Anyway, I need to talk to you about something else."

Something in his tone changes my whole lighthearted attitude. Swinging my legs back to the floor, I sit up straighter. "What is it?"

"It's about what happened this morning."

I stare at him, my mind still wrapped in Donald Douglas's story.

"With Violet and the bathroom," Perry adds.

"Oh! That."

"Yeah, *that*," he says, annoyed. "Look, Violet's still really embarrassed about it. She was nervous about spending the night anyway because of…our situation and I told her it was going to be okay. But then this morning you got a front row view of her bare butt."

"It wasn't bare!"

His finger shoots out accusingly. "Which means you *did* see it!"

"Not on purpose! Besides, it's a tiny apartment. Stuff like that is bound to happen. I'll try to stay out of your way in the future, but she's going to have to get used to it."

Perry's shaking his head before I even finish. "No, Ash. I want her to feel comfortable here. *You've* certainly gotten comfortable. Maybe *too* comfortable."

"What does that mean?"

"It means…" He takes a deep breath. "This isn't working anymore."

I try to lighten the mood—and relieve the growing sense of anxiety ready to flood through me. "Are you breaking up with me?"

"Ash, I'm serious. Our living situation was never supposed to be permanent. You were just going to stay with me for a few days until we found—"

"My family?" All lightness flies out the window now that I can tell that he's serious. "Well, guess what? We found my last remaining relative and he's a giant dick."

"Please don't get mad."

Getting to my feet, I start collecting my clothes and stuffing them in the bag I still have from my stay at Vernon's house.

Chapter Six

"Why would I get mad? I have a *million* places I can go! Oh and money? Not an issue whatsoever. There are people all over town dying to hire an unqualified amnesiac from the 60s!"

"Now you're just being ridiculous." Still, he doesn't get up to prevent me from hastily throwing my things into my bag. "You found an under-the-table job before. You'll find another one."

"You don't—" I'm cut off by the sound of my cell phone ringing from the couch. It must've fallen out of my pocket while I was laying there. Shooting a nasty look to Perry, I snatch it up and answer it. "Hello?"

"It's Harkness," she says in her no-nonsense voice. "There's been a murder. And he looks an awful lot like you."

Chapter Seven
ASH

After stepping off the bus that brought me across town, I walk the few extra blocks toward the charred remains of the Ellsworth Science and Technology Research laboratory. It's a reminder of where my invasion into the personal lives of Perry and Rachel started. And Vernon. He and his family paid the ultimate sacrifice for my arrival.

The bag slung over my shoulder is heavier than I thought it would be. Perry told me I didn't have to pack up right away, but with the way I was already making a dramatic exit, my pride wouldn't let me come back to collect my things. Besides, it's not like I had a lot to pack anyway. All of my personal belongings fit into one duffel bag.

Peeling my eyes away from the ruins of the lab, I cross the street and approach the police line. Officer Lawson spots me and calls to Detective Harkness.

"You called in your witness?" he asks.

Turning, she sees me and marches my way. "Let him in."

Chapter Seven

Officer Lawson holds the police tape up for me to pass underneath and I drop my bag near the line. "You mind watching this while I talk to her?"

Glancing down at the bag, he looks back at me with disapproval, but doesn't say anything.

"Thanks!" I tell him, just before Harkness approaches.

"Come take a look before the M.E. gets here." She leads me over toward the gate in the chain-link fence where an ominous white sheet covers a body. To the right of the sheet I notice blood splatter on the dusty ground, immediately making me feel the severity of the situation.

Pulling back the sheet with powder blue latex gloves, Harkness reveals the victim. Young male, blond, same build as me. He lays face-down on the ground and his gray hoodie is stained with blood from the large tear near the center of his back, revealing contorted flesh beneath. I avert my eyes for a moment, but the image is still present in my head. Better to take a good look so we can figure out what happened.

Harkness starts reading off the stats in a very business-like tone, unaware of my discomfort. "We found his driver's license on him. His name is Peter Jones. Twenty-something male, stabbed three times with an object approximately three inches wide. Once in the back, twice in the front. One of those attacks went straight through his heart."

Despite everything I've done—and seen—as Heat, this is by far the most gruesome.

"Judging by the trail of footprints coming down the path from the top of the mountain, we suspect he might've been hiking, even though this trail is supposed to be locked up," she goes on. "Someone must've broken the lock."

I look up at the gate. Rachel, Perry, and I broke the lock when we went up to explore the cave. Someone died as a result of that outing too. All because of my brother's vendetta against me. He needs to be stopped.

Harkness points down to the dusty ground again. "When we got here, foot tracks showed evidence of a scuffle, which makes us believe he was jumped. That part's obvious because it's not like he stabbed himself." She turns and motions up to the trees and other overgrowth surrounding the entrance. "There are several hiding spots in this area so it's quite possible someone was waiting for him. And with this end of the city being mainly industrial, the number of potential witnesses are extremely few."

I force myself to look directly at Harkness, yet my eyes keep wandering to the body. "What do you know about the killer?"

"Judging by the number of stab wounds and the evidence of a fight, we think this might've been the perp's first time killing. Or one of them. But the fact that Jones was jumped suggests that it was a premeditated attack—even if sloppily done." She points down to the victim again. "The way he's lying and the heavier blood stains on his back suggests he was struck from behind first, between the ribs. It doesn't appear to be deep, but it's certainly not superficial. On his front there are two more wounds, one of those being the fatal strike."

"Through the heart?"

She nods. "Uh-huh."

On the other side of the police tape a man in a loose-fitting gray suit carrying a briefcase steps through. His bald head suggests he's in the later part of middle-age. Although we're standing at a crime scene—a murder scene—his expression is blank. Even a little bored.

"That's the medical examiner," Harkness tells me. "He'll have to confirm all my theories, but I've seen enough of these in my career to piece together what happened." She puts her hand on my arm and guides me off to the side. "Let's talk over here. There's more."

"More?" I ask. "Do you know who the killer is?"

"Not conclusively," she says. "But I have a strong theory."

"Who?"

"Donald Douglas."

"Douglas? I thought he was in police custody?"

"He *was…*" She sighs.

"He escaped?"

"Somehow. And what's weirder is that earlier today he started hurting himself—"

"How?" I interrupt.

"Scratching up his arms, from what the guard tells me. Like a nervous tic. Really bad, I guess."

"If Watkins's theory holds up and Douglas is the one who took his daughter, maybe he's feeling guilty."

"Or maybe he's *worried* about his daughter," she says. "No matter the state of his mind at this traumatic moment, he's still a father."

"True."

"Anyway, they put him in a straitjacket and gave him a sedative to calm him down and when they went to give him dinner he was gone."

"Gone?"

"Nowhere to be found," she says. "Nobody checked him out or even visited him. I mean, if he really is from the 60s, he wouldn't know anyone here anyway."

My mind is already placing the blame for the jailbreak on someone in particular, but I decide to hear Harkness out before I give my suggestion.

"And get this," she adds. "Security footage shows a man in a trench coat suddenly in his cell with him."

"So you saw him?" My voice raises excitedly.

She shakes her head. "No. Thanks to budget restrictions, we only have one camera to watch two cells. So there's a corner of Douglas's cell that's not visible on surveillance footage. We only saw part of the man in the trench coat."

"And I'm guessing the corner you couldn't see is where the man in trench coat was?"

"Mm-hmm. After that, Douglas was gone. Any thoughts?"

I nod. "Yeah, this is all probably the work of the Gatekeeper—Arlus Cain. Directly or indirectly. I mean, it's probably a pretty good bet that the Gatekeeper is the one who freed him. What he said to him then is anybody's guess." Resting my hands on my hips, I curse lightly to myself.

She sighs and glances back at the medical examiner looking over the victim. "I know. I was afraid something like this might happen. Dealing with supers is too unpredictable."

Nodding over to the body, I ask, "Why do you think this was the work of Donald Douglas?"

"He hated you when he saw you," she says.

"I don't know if I'd say *hated*—"

"No, he was just anxious around Lawson and Watkins, but when he saw you he wanted to kill you," she says. "Which is very telling. It means that he either knows you or thinks he knows you."

"And he attacked this guy here because he thought it was me?"

She shrugs. "It's the best answer I've been able to come up with so far. We have to look into this case a bit more because on first glance there doesn't seem to be anything connecting the two. Especially since Douglas isn't even from this time period. And it certainly wasn't random. Or a gang initiation. Ellsworth doesn't really have any gang activity—of course, that could change if we get more supers that the police can't even fight."

"Maybe it was drugs or something," I muse, not really believing it myself.

"We'll check all possible scenarios, but the vic doesn't seem like the drug-using—or dealing—type. My money's on Douglas and the Gatekeeper. What did you say his powers were again?"

"Opening portals," I say. "But what's weird is that every time he's thrown *me* through a portal, I've come out instantly on the other side, just somewhere else."

"What are you saying?"

"I'm saying that if you gave Douglas sedatives, wouldn't he still be groggy by the time he killed your victim?"

"Maybe that's why it took three stab wounds to do the trick."

"Unless the Gatekeeper took Douglas somewhere where he could sleep off the sedative before he told him to hunt me down."

"Like time travel or something?"

I shrug. "I don't know. Maybe."

"Isn't that…a little *too* weird? Even for you."

"Yeah, but the truth of the matter is that I somehow went fifty years without aging and Douglas somehow went from being sedated to being able to jump a young man and kill him in a matter of a few hours. Time doesn't seem to be linear when it comes to the Gatekeeper. And that's not to mention that Douglas claims he's from 1969."

Harkness rubs her eyes with her thumb and index finger. "Okay, well, this conversation is once again going beyond my realm of reality, so I'm going to bring it back down to my level. Time travel aside, is this area familiar to you at all that Douglas—or the Gatekeeper—would assume you'd be here?"

Without hesitation, I nod. "Yeah. The old coal mine is where I was when I first woke up in 2019." Pointing over across the street, I add, "And what's left of the lab is where I first went when I got down to the city. It's also where I first saw the Gatekeeper during the fire storm."

"I was afraid of that," she says.

"Why?"

"It means there's a good chance that you're the target. It also means that you going anywhere else that you spend a significant amount of time could be where they strike next. I need you to give me a list of places you frequent. Where you live, where you go during the day, where you shop, all of it, especially if you've been going to other people's houses. Give me their names too. I need to make sure you and everyone you interact with are protected."

My mind flashes to Perry and Rachel. I don't want to give their names to the police but I also don't want them to get hurt because of me. I don't really have a choice with this.

"I'll get you a list," I tell her.

"And I want you in protective custody."

"No! I can take care of myself. Besides, with the Gatekeeper's powers, if he wants me, he can get me."

"Yeah, but *we* want the Gatekeeper too—or Arlus Cain, rather. Isn't that what you agreed to? We were going to try to *legally* get him behind bars. We can't do that if we can't find him."

"And until we have a cell that can contain him—or evidence against him to put him there—we're really just trying to keep him from hurting anyone else," I counter. "Which means I need to be able to move about without an entourage."

She motions over to the victim. "Look what good that's done so far."

That stings.

Picking up on it, Harkness says, "I didn't mean to—you didn't know this was going to happen. Look, I just want to make sure you're going to be okay and this is the best way I know how. We do this with anyone who might be a target. I just want a police car sitting outside your home. That's it. You don't have to have coffee with them in the morning or even wave to them when you see them. Just think of it as another car parked on the street."

"Yeah, there's only one problem with that."

"What's that?" she asks.

"I don't really have a home right now."

She narrows her eyes. "So where have you been staying?"

"With a friend, but he just kicked me out."

Looking up to Officer Lawson, she asks me, "Is that why you have the bag?"

Chapter Seven

"Yep."

"So where are you going to stay tonight?"

I look down and sigh heavily, buying time to weigh my few options. "I think I can probably stay with another friend of mine. But I haven't asked her yet."

"Well anywhere is better than nowhere. Especially with someone trying to hurt you. Get me the names and addresses of both places so we can keep them both under watch tonight. Lawson!" she calls over my shoulder. "Can you please escort Ash here back home? We're going to be keeping an eye on him until further notice."

I glare at her, but she simply smiles back.

"It's for your own protection."

Chapter Eight

ASH

Rachel's standing on the front step outside her front door before I'm even out of the back of the police car. I offer a thanks to Officer Lawson as he opens the door for me and sling my dusty bag over my shoulder before walking up the driveway to meet Rachel. Luckily, Evan's car isn't anywhere to be seen. Not that that means he's not here.

"What's this?" She points toward the street. Officer Lawson clumsily tries to turn around the police car to get a parking spot across the street with a better view of the house.

I stare at the car a minute, watch as Lawson maneuvers around two other parked cars before settling against the opposite curb. I turn back to Rachel. "Uh…let's go inside and talk."

"Ash…" she warns.

"I'll tell you in a minute." Anything I can do to get the eyes off of me. It's been twenty minutes since Harkness put me under police supervision and I'm already sick of it.

With disapproval in her eyes, Rachel holds the door open

for me as I step through. Inside, I drop my bag by the door and immediately step over to the living room to close the curtains. The sun will be setting in the next hour, meaning the police would otherwise have a front-row-seat inside the house. Talk about creepy.

"Are you going to tell me what's going on?" She stands behind the couch with her arms crossed. "You're freaking me out."

"Well, I don't mean to alarm you, but there *may* be a crazy man trying to hunt me down to kill me."

"*Kill* you? Ash, what happened? Who is this guy?"

After peering through the curtains one more time and seeing that Lawson is playing on his phone, I turn back to her and dive into the story of my day, leaving out the part about Perry and my immediate eviction.

"So this Donald guy thinks it's 1969?" she asks, less agitated than she was when I arrived. "Just like when you disappeared."

"Yeah." I take a seat on the chair closest to the window and pull back the curtain again to peer out. The sun glare is blinding. In half an hour the intense rays will be obscured by the mountains to the west of the city.

"And he wants to kill you to save his daughter from the Gatekeeper?"

"Allegedly," I say. "It makes the most sense to us and that's the direction Harkness is exploring, but she's also got people investigating Donald Douglas and the possibility that *he's* the one responsible for his daughter's disappearance."

"But if he really is from the past, the only record she'll be able to pull up will be his from the 60s," Rachel says. "Like she did when you were arrested."

"*Questioned*," I correct. "There was no arrest."

"Do you want to know what I think?"

"Always."

A bashful smile springs to her face and she tries to ignore it. "I think the Gatekeeper's powers allow him to time travel."

"Time travel? Rach, that's not poss—"

"Not possible?" She hooks an eyebrow. "Ash, you especially have seen enough to know that anything is possible. Besides, what other explanation do you have?"

I shrug.

"Let's pretend your arrival was a surprise to the Gatekeeper, which is almost certain because we know the Gatekeeper turned Vernon into Black Magnet and that didn't happen until *after* you showed up," she says. "But let's say for the sake of argument that you were unexpected to him. That means he thought that you had died or gone somewhere that you'd never escape from. And we already know you two have history. It was probably a fight between the two of you that caused your disappearance."

"Rach, the point?"

"If you could escape from wherever you were for the last fifty years, why couldn't Donald Douglas?" she finally asks. "He was brought in by the police because he was essentially just scared that he didn't know where he was. If he really intended to hurt that woman he grabbed because he's a killer, the person he supposedly killed at the gate for the old coal mine would've been a woman, not someone who had the same features as you."

"That's if he was following the same pattern," I say.

"Which he's not. And that's very telling."

"So you're saying he's trying to kill me too?"

"Yes, and the Gatekeeper plucked him out of 1969 to do it."

"I still don't see it."

Frustrated, she comes around and sits on the edge of the couch. "I think fifty years ago Arlus didn't realize that *he's* the one who made you disappear—wherever it was that you disappeared to. It wasn't until you *came back* that he realized the extent of his powers, got it? Maybe the reason we haven't seen him since the fire at ESTR is because he's been practicing his powers and seeing what he can do with them. Maybe he found out how to time travel."

"He had the last fifty years to practice."

"Yes, but he didn't know he needed to practice because you weren't around," she says. "He hates you and he thought you were dead. When he saw you not only alive and well, but *young*, it got him thinking of the possibilities. Your brother is not a stupid man."

"If only he was," I mutter. "But I still think he knew some of what he could do with his powers. I mean, the people who were investigating the car crash that killed Arlus's daughter just disappeared after Vernon agreed to be his bitch. That was probably his powers."

"Maybe."

"Unless he just didn't need his powers that much in the last fifty years," I say. "Not until I returned. That set him off and now he's exploring the full extent of his powers, just as I've done. He's powerful and I don't know exactly what he's capable of. But, first thing's first: we still need to figure out why he hates me."

"You haven't remembered anything else?" she asks.

"No. And now even Harkness is on me about that. She says that our sibling rivalry is hurting innocent people and until I remember what the cause of it is, more people are likely to get hurt—or die. She has a point, but it still doesn't help me any."

"Nothing new has come up?" she asks.

I shake my head. "No. More and more things are familiar to me, but details and a lot of my relationships with friends and stuff are still just kind of…foggy."

"Wasn't Perry working on something to help you remember? Or replay your visions or something?"

I shake my head. "I don't want to talk to Perry right now."

Rachel chips the paint off her fingernails. "Is that why you brought a bag?"

"Yeah."

"What happened?" She shoots me a look and continues with her nails.

"I guess his girlfriend didn't like the idea of his friend bumming it on the couch."

"So he asked you to move out?" Her eyes grow wide.

"Yeah. I mean, he didn't say it had to be immediate, but I was mad." I let out a deep breath. "So I left."

"I'm surprised." She brushes off the chipped paint from her legs. "I thought for sure he would've picked his friend over his girlfriend. I'll have to talk to him."

"Don't. It's fine. I'll figure it out. And I get what he's saying. It *is* a small apartment and this *wasn't* supposed to be a long-term arrangement, but it still sucks."

"Yeah." She drums her fingers on her leg.

We're quiet. I peek through the curtains again. The sun is now only just barely visible above the mountains. Like an orange globe sitting just beyond the rocky horizon, casting the sky into shades of reds and pinks.

"Well," Rachel says suddenly, "my house always did make the most sense for a houseguest anyway."

My head snaps back to her. "No, that's not what I was saying. I can find—"

"Ash, please. You don't have anywhere else to go. And besides, it makes the most sense. I have the extra bedroom. It might be further away from downtown, but it'll certainly be more comfortable for you. You'll have your own space."

"Are you sure?" Better not to let myself get too excited.

She thinks about it a minute, then says, "Yeah. I should've offered right from the beginning. You're my friend and you need help right now. And, like I said, I have the space."

"What about…Evan?" I ask timidly. "What's he going to say?"

"Uh…well, why don't we just keep this between us for a bit?" she says. "I'll have to think of a good way to tell him."

"I don't think he likes me."

"No, it's not that," she says quickly. "He's just…protective of me."

"Do you like that?"

She shrugs. "It's just a part of his character that I've grown used to."

"That's not really an answer to the question."

Rachel sighs. "Do I wish he didn't get so angry so easily? Sure. Do I wish he wasn't as jealous as he can sometimes get? Absolutely. But I know he does it all because he cares about me."

Sounds like he's trying to control you, I think, but keep that to myself.

"How are you doing?" I ask. "With everything. I know before you said you were feeling kind of *meh.*"

Lifting her hand behind the back of her blonde hair, she scratches her neck and looks off at nothing in particular.

"Um…not much has changed, I guess. Still only mildly satisfied with my job. And I love this house, but every day I'm stressing out about paying for it. I'm barely scraping by as it is."

I feel a twinge of guilt for basically inviting myself to be her new roommate. Especially since I have no way to offer her anything toward rent. This isn't a good time for her to be dishing out charity and I'm a grown man. I should be able to support myself.

"Evan's given up about trying to get me to go out," she goes on. "I think he's finally learned that I don't have any money. And that adds another layer to my stress because then I feel guilty for not being able to do the things that he wants to do." She sighs and adds with a half-hearted chuckle, "My life's a mess."

"Trust me, you're doing a lot better than me."

"Am I, though?"

"What do you mean?"

"You're likable," she says. "And since you're not sure who you're supposed to be, you become whoever you need to be whenever the need arises."

"Yeah, but that also makes me feel like I'm spiraling out of control sometimes without anything to secure my confidence."

The closest thing I have to that is Linda telling me that I've always been someone to stand up for what's right.

Running her hands through her hair absently, she goes on, "I don't know. Sometimes I wonder if I'm better off just starting over from scratch."

"What do you mean?"

"Cut ties with everyone and everything I'm associated with. Sell my house. Quit my job. Find a new career. A new city. A new passion."

My heart rate picks up at the thought of losing her—especially to such a haphazard plan. If it could even be called a 'plan.'

"That's not very smart," I say bluntly. "You have a job. You have a beautiful house that you're proud of. Just take a step back and reevaluate. Maybe there are only certain people that need to be trimmed out of your life."

She smirks, picking up on where I'm heading. "Like Evan?"

Turning back to the window, I peer outside. Since it's mid-October, dusk has set in earlier than usual. The police officer's face across the street is lit up with the glow of his phone.

When I look over at Rachel again, she's noticeably quiet.

"Are you thinking about breaking up with him?"

My question hangs in the air for several long, excruciating seconds.

"No," she finally says. "I'm not going to break up with him on a whim. He deserves better than that."

Trying to hide my disappointment, I tell her, "You shouldn't make any major decisions quickly. It's not who you are and it's probably not going to make you happier. Better to look for other fresh starts in your life before you go burning bridges."

"Yeah—"

Buried in my pocket, my phone chirps with an alert from the police scanner app I had Perry download. I pull it out and open the app in time to hear a voice say, "We're in pursuit of a seemingly mentally unfit male on Hickory Avenue, heading south. We believe he's tied to a prior murder."

Chapter Eight

Donald Douglas.

Standing, I start pulling at my shirt, revealing the Heat suit beneath.

"Ash, what're you doing?" Rachel asks. "The police are right outside!"

"I have to go, Rach." Pulling on my mask and gloves, I open the back sliding door. "Don't lock me out!"

Before she has a chance to say anything, I burst into flames and shoot up into the darkening night sky.

Chapter Nine

Detective Harkness

"Stand down," Harkness barks into the radio as Detective Watkins navigates the car through the tight city streets mere blocks from where Peter Jones was found. "We're on our way."

Sitting in the passenger seat, grasping on to the handle above the door as Watkins rounds the corners faster than he normally would, Harkness can't help but feel useless sitting here waiting until they arrive at the scene. If only the department wasn't so full of male egos that would let a woman drive her own damn car.

But there isn't any time to argue about it. Officer Greene spotted Donald Douglas while they were canvassing the area and cornered him in a large warehouse building on West Jefferson Street. The alert went out to all available units and even now, as Watkins races to the warehouse, other officers are on their way to join them.

Screeching to a stop among a queue of other police cars

strewn all over West Jefferson, Harkness hops out of the car with her gun pointed in the air and shuffles in a crouched position to the first uniform she lays eyes on.

"Catch me up." She takes a knee beside him.

He waits half a second for Detective Watkins to join them before he says, "The suspect is inside somewhere, but we have men—*people*—guarding every possible exit. Officer Greene chased him down and Officers—"

"Son of a bitch!" Harkness calls out, her eyes pointed to the air above them.

Soaring through the night sky like a rocket is a man on fire, flying straight toward the building.

Heat.

She watches as he lands right in front of the myriad of police cars and his flames diffuse. She notices Officer Greene and Detective Watkins aiming their weapons at him. Looking around, she sees that anyone who has a badge is doing the same thing.

Snatching the walkie talkie from her belt, she shouts into it, "Stand down! I repeat, *stand down!* Don't shoot!" With a shaking hand gripping the walkie, she watches gratefully as several people retract their guns to a defensive position. She breathes a sigh of relief and rehooks the walkie before stepping forward. "Greene, you're coming in with me."

"The hell you are!" Watkins says.

Ignoring him, Harkness calls over to the officer at the next car. "Lyons! You're with me too. Stay alert, stay together, and let's clear each room as we move through. Got it? Nobody shoots. We need to bring Douglas in for more questioning and we need him alive to do that."

"Jenna!" Watkins yells.

Spinning on her heels, she steps uncomfortably close to him. "It's *Detective Harkness*, Walter." Turning toward the building again, she calls out to Greene and Lyons, "Let's go!"

Wide eyes and confused looks surround them. Ignoring

them all, Harkness, Greene, and Lyons all run into the building, guns pointed toward the sky, ready to use them if need be.

"Detective," Watkins calls after her, but she proceeds as if she doesn't hear him. "Detective Harkness!"

Leaving the safety of the surrounding police cars, Harkness and her makeshift team approach the front door and smoothly pop inside, away from the chaos on the street. The front entrance leads into an office space. It's dark, but thanks to the night outside, it doesn't take long for Harkness's eyes to adjust.

Room-by-room, the trio secure the front offices and radio out to one of the patrols outside to come in and hold their positions while they secure the rest of the building.

Through the doors at the end of the main hallway, they step out into the cavernous warehouse. Ten-feet tall shelves line the space, filled with boxes and totes and other large storage containers. Each row creates aisles upon aisles of potential hiding places. There's no easy way to do one quick sweep of the area.

Harkness steps closer to Greene and Lyons and lowers her voice as she doles out orders. "Greene, you stick to the outside. Lyons, you secure the main aisle. I'm going to move between the shorter aisles. Call out if you hear anything."

They each nod and disperse in the directions she gives them. Pulling out her flashlight, she extends out both hands in front of her. Her gun in one and her flashlight in the other. The light only helps slightly to ease her racing heart. If her gut is right, they're looking for a murderer who might not hesitate to kill again, even if she is a cop.

Harkness steps carefully, doing her best to anticipate any oncoming attacks while simultaneously kicking herself for not pulling on her bullet-proof vest on the ride over. Although if Douglas is carrying a weapon, the likelihood of it being a gun is slim based off of the murder by the gate.

Across the room, she hears footsteps moving quickly, getting fainter with each step. Running away. And it's definitely not either of her guys because they'd call if they got something.

Breaking into her own run, Harkness tries to keep pace with the footsteps while also trying to determine just how many aisles down the footsteps are coming from.

She reaches the end of the aisle and cuts right, running along the far wall and waving the flashlight in front of her. Catching sight of a red pant leg, she knows immediately that it's Heat.

"That stupid idiot," she murmurs to herself before clicking off the light and pursuing him.

Just as she's rounding the corner down the aisle Heat was, one of the tall shelves crashes at the end, blocking her path. Coming to a halt, she spins to race around the aisle as quick as she can, her feet moving faster when she hears Greene shouting, "Freeze, police!"

Harkness breaks into an all-out sprint as more crashing sounds emanate from that end of the building. Just as she's approaching, she feels a cool breeze on her face.

An open door.

The next instant, light erupts in the dark space as Heat volleys several attacks in the opposite direction. The light shows Greene on the floor, scooting backward on his butt. Surprised by the sight, but otherwise fine.

"You okay?" she calls to him as she comes to the end of the aisle. She backs up immediately from the intense heat of the flames. Like standing next to a giant bonfire. She reaches for her officer and helps him to his feet.

"I'm good, Detective," Greene responds, taking several careful steps backward. "Just fell."

"Good," she says quickly. "Stay back."

Now completely on fire, Heat hovers in the air between whoever he faces and Detective Harkness.

Watching as another fireball rises in his fiery palm, Harkness slams her flashlight against the nearest shelving, hoping that the cacophony of echoing metal is enough to get his attention. As an added effort, she barks out, "Hey!"

It does the trick. The flame in Heat's hand stifles as he turns around to look at her. The next moment, Douglas runs through the open doors and outside.

"Suspect is fleeing on foot," Greene says into his walkie. "Out the back entrance."

Heat moves to follow Douglas, but Harkness calls out to him. "Heat! Don't you dare do it. I *will* shoot you if that's what it takes."

"Copy that," Watkins says from the other end of the walkie. "We're moving in."

The flames consuming Heat rise higher, lifting him up into the air as well. A moment later, they subside slowly enough for him to land on his feet and then disappear all at once.

"Officer Greene, go help track down Douglas before he gets too far." Harkness's eyes remain firmly locked on Heat. "I'll be fine."

The officer hesitates a moment, but runs off past Heat and out the doors in pursuit of the runaway suspect.

"What the hell were you thinking?" she yells at Heat once Greene has left. "That was stupid!"

"I was trying to get him into custody faster than you guys could've!" he counters.

"That's a lie. You were catering to your enormous ego, which was hurt because I had an officer sit outside your door to *babysit* you."

"Ego or not, my way would've gotten the job done."

"Would it have? How did you know Douglas didn't get his hands on a gun?"

"He would've pulled one on me if he did!"

"What would've happened if you got shot?"

He crosses his arms. "I didn't get shot."

"And that fire show you did? Do you even know what this warehouse is used for? How could you be sure that there wasn't anything flammable in here?"

"The building's still standing."

"Yeah, but what if it wasn't? You didn't *think*! Your actions were shortsighted and could've gotten people hurt. Or worse. I have half a mind to arrest you right now for obstruction."

"You wouldn't."

"Try me."

He drops his arms and changes the subject. "So now what do we do since Douglas got away?"

"Hope that my team is able to find him."

"And how are they going to fare against someone who might have a gun?"

"Better than you," she says. "They've had training."

"Better hope that's all they need. The odds are pretty good that Douglas is a murderer. What's to say he won't kill someone else before *you* can get to him? After all—following your logic again—he could have a gun now. And if he's shooting his victims, that changes the method and screws up your probable cause with the last victim, doesn't it?"

"I'm not going to sit here and have an argument with you about what's right and wrong because the difference is, *I'm* the police officer and *you're* the one running around in a mask."

"Someone that *you* recruited to help! *Let* me help!"

She puts her hands on her hips and studies him, realizing that this argument isn't going anywhere.

"Detective Harkness," someone calls from behind her.

She ignores it, too fired up with the argument.

"This conversation is over," she tells Heat. "I have work to do now that you've gone and screwed up what might've been our only opportunity to get Douglas back into custody."

"Custody that he would've escaped from again," Heat says.

She lets out a deep breath, doing her best to release all the anger building up inside her. It doesn't work. "I suggest you go home, unless you're waiting for another police escort?"

The Gatekeeper

The question hangs in the air for a moment. In their silence, Officer Lyons calls her name one more time.

"Detective Harkness, you need to come look at this."

"What is it, Officer?" she snaps.

"I think I might've found the murder weapon used on Peter Jones."

Chapter Ten

ASH

Detective Harkness and I rush over to Officer Lyons, who is crouching beside a shelf. He points his flashlight at our feet as we approach before turning it to the small gap between the bottom shelf and the floor.

Pulling out her own flashlight, Harkness asks, "What is it?"

"Take a look." Lyons points toward the floor. Beneath the bottom shelf lays a short switchblade just barely visible in the dust and shadows. Dried blood coats the end of it, with splatter marks along the handle.

"If it wasn't for the reflection of the blade, I wouldn't have noticed it," he says.

"Did you call for CSI?" she asks.

He shakes his head. "No, but I'll get on that."

"Good. We'll need to get this smudge on here tested as well. Confirm that it's blood and that it belonged to Peter Jones. Go and notify them outside. I want to take a closer look. Good work, Officer."

Lyons's eyes linger on me a moment, but he decides not to question why I get to stick around and he doesn't. When he's gone, I ask, "Are you sure that's it?"

Sinking into a crouch, Harkness leans forward and holds two fingers just along the edge of the weapon, careful not to touch it. "The size of the blade seems consistent with Peter Jones's wounds." She leans in closer, resting her knee on the cement floor and peering at it with her face close. "There isn't any dust on it, unlike everything else under the shelf. And although it's dry, the blood—or unknown reddish, brown substance—seems fresh. It hasn't been here long." She sits up straighter, still studying it. "Did you see Douglas with it at all?"

I consider lying to save my pride but decide against it. That's not going to help us catch this guy. "Honestly, the light from my own flames was so bright that I didn't see."

Looking over her shoulder she glares at me.

"CSI is on their way," Lyons says through Harkness's walkie.

"Copy that," she replies into it.

"CSI is going to come in and take pictures?" I ask.

"Yeah. If you want to get out of here so they don't question you, now's probably the best time."

"What about Officer Lyons?"

"I'll worry about him," she says. "You go. After all, you are the one responsible for our prime suspect getting away."

I bite back my retort and instead say, "I at least want copies of any pictures you guys take of the weapon."

"I'm not sure I can authorize that," she says. "That'd be releasing evidence to the public."

"But I'm not the public."

"A—Heat…" she says as a warning.

"No, you're the one who agreed to bring me on as an informant," I counter, my voice growing. "Every time there's a case involving a super, I need to be clued in on what's happening."

She rises to her feet and crosses her arms over her chest. "We haven't confirmed that this is a case involving a super."

"Oh, come on!" I shout. "Don't sabotage this case just because you're mad at me! I'm sorry I didn't use my head earlier. You were right. Unlike you, I didn't go through police training." I pause, waiting for her to say something, but she doesn't. From the main doors at the front of the building, I hear the entourage of policemen from outside barreling in.

"You should go," she finally says. "Before they get here and we both wind up in trouble."

"Okay, but remember: by withholding information from me you could be sending someone else who looks like me straight to the grave."

Without waiting for her to respond, I turn and run down the aisle toward the door Douglas escaped through, deciding not to use flames. That would only draw attention.

———

LANDING AS SOFT as I can in Rachel's backyard still leaves the grass singed beneath me when the flames dissipate. Another way I'm not starting off on the right foot with this living arrangement, especially when all I have to offer is my winning smile and killer personality.

Inside, the smell of sauce hits me immediately, with the cooking tomatoes, garlic, and spices all mixing together to bring that familiar sense of *home* as soon as I step through the door. I'm surprised to see Perry sitting at the kitchen counter, his hands clutching a black mug of coffee.

"Oh good, you're back," Rachel says from the stove. Steam rises from the pot she's cooking at. "I invited Perry over for pasta and I wasn't sure if you would be back in time to have some."

I pull off my mask and gloves. "It smells delicious." Glancing over at Perry, I ask, "Where's Violet?"

"Working."

"Figured you two would want to get a jump start on moving in together," I mutter.

"Enough of that," Rachel says quickly. One-by-one she sets three steaming bowls on the counter. "Ash, sit down so we can eat."

Begrudgingly, I take the spot to Perry's right while Rachel takes the one to his left.

"She's not moving in." Perry blows on the pasta as he twirls it up in his fork.

"That's what it sounded like earlier."

"We just want space and there isn't enough in that tiny apartment."

"Doesn't she have an apartment?" I ask. "Or doesn't she sleep at all?"

"Ash, don't be rude," Rachel warns.

"Yeah, don't make this personal," he says. "I never said you needed to move out *today* and I knew you'd have a place to go. I'm sorry if you felt like I was choosing Violet over you. That's not what I intended."

"Whatever." I stare down at my food. "I'm not even mad about it anymore. I have bigger problems to deal with." Based off of my attitude, we all know it's a lie, but they both let it slide. Rachel probably talked to him about it even though I told her not to.

"What did you rush out of here so quickly for earlier?" Rachel asks, likely eager to change the subject.

"You know how I said that I'm the target for a killer?"

"Seriously?" Perry asks with wide eyes.

"That's looking more and more true," I say, ignoring him.

"What happened? Are you okay?" She leans forward to look at me around Perry.

"I'm fine, but that call I ran out for earlier was for Donald Douglas."

"The man who killed someone who looks just like you?" she asks.

Chapter Ten

"That's the one."

Perry looks between us, confused. "Is this the guy who think it's 1969?"

"Yes," I say curtly. "Anyway, the police found him at a warehouse only a few blocks away from the crime scene. There were police everywhere by the time I arrived, but none of them were running in—"

"Probably waiting until they sealed off the exits," Perry interrupts.

I take my next bite and swallow it quickly so I can continue. "*Anyway*," I say more forcefully, "I went in, chased him down. He popped open the emergency exit, but I managed to pull him back inside—less room for him to run. I went full-on Heat mode to try to scare him, you know?"

"Ash, you didn't hurt him, did you?" Rachel asks.

"No. Detective Harkness distracted me before I could make my move and by the time I turned back around, Douglas was gone."

"Why wouldn't she let you get him?" Perry asks.

"Was she afraid you would hurt him?" Rachel adds.

Looking down at my food again, I poke around at it with unnecessary vigor. "No. She said I didn't know what was in the building and I could've started the place on fire."

"Well…" she says.

"But I didn't!" I say quickly.

She nods. "That's good."

I know she's only trying to pacify me, but I take it regardless. "Anyway, we got into it and I'm pretty sure she's mad at me. But it sounds like they found the murder weapon, so that's good."

They're both quiet, which pulls my attention toward them.

"What?" I snap.

"Well…" Perry starts, but thinks better of it.

"You *did* accidentally start a building on fire before—in the same area," Rachel points out. "Remember the old coal mine plant that was covered with combustibles?"

"That was a fluke thing," I counter. "Back when I didn't know what I was doing."

"It's been—what?—three months since then?" Perry asks. "You know more now, sure, but sometimes it doesn't hurt to get a reminder now and then."

"And people make mistakes," she adds. "Sometimes we act before we really think. It's not a bad thing to remember to be careful sometimes."

"Whatever," I say, turning back to my food. "Either way, Douglas is still out there."

"Even so, someone running around who thinks it's still the 60s is going to stick out like a sore thumb," he says. "And if he's going around killing people, that'll draw attention too."

"And if he's scared because of what's going on with his daughter—or even just being in a different time period—he might be hanging out at places that are familiar to him," she adds. "Places that have been around since his time. That might be a good place to start."

"That's not a bad idea." I pop another bite in my mouth and note that Rachel and Perry have both finished their meals. I've been talking, which has slowed me down.

Pushing her bowl aside, Rachel gets up and retrieves her laptop from by the couch and retakes her seat beside Perry. "We can figure this out with a little bit of work."

"You're going to search through every place in the city that's been around for fifty years?" he asks.

"Well no," she says. "He's on foot, so he won't be able to get too far, which narrows our search. It's getting later, but it's not so late that he'd want to find a place to stay for the night. Especially not with the police following him. But he's probably getting hungry, which means he'll be finding a place to eat. And Ash, you said he looks kind of grungy?"

"Yeah," I say in between the final bites of my meal. "Almost like someone who could have a mental disorder. That's what the police first thought, anyway."

"Which means he'd stick out in any sort of classy restaurant," she says. "Not that there are a lot of them in that part of the city."

"So what does that leave us?" Perry asks.

"Bars, mostly. But bars that serve food."

"And they have to have been around for a long time," I add. "Or something that looks close enough."

"I'll do my best," she says.

"And quickly," I add. "He probably doesn't have any money, so it might be a dine and ditch."

"Even more reason to think it's a bar." Perry turns to me. "Are you sure you don't remember anything that might be helpful? Any indication why Arlus would be annoyed with you? Or even who this Douglas guy is?"

"No."

He sighs. "That sucks. If you could remember, it'd save us a lot of time."

"Um, I seem to recall *you* saying you were working on a device to let me see my visions more clearly. Whatever happened to that?"

"I got busy with other things," he says. "The research is all there and I have most of the component parts, it's just a matter of fitting it all together."

I stare at him, hoping he'd take the hint without my prompting. "You said Violet was working tonight, right?"

His eyes grow large. "You want me to go *now*?"

"You said it yourself, Perry, we don't have a lot of time!"

"It's almost eight o'clock!"

"Please?"

Sighing again as he gets to his feet, he says, "Fine. But only because I feel bad that I kicked you out."

"So you admit that you *did* kick me out!"

"I never said it was immediate!" he counters.

"Would you boys knock it off!" Rachel shouts over us. "I'm trying to focus."

Perry and I smirk at each other, the resentment built up toward one another now officially faded.

"I'll let you know what I come up with," he says, stepping to the door. "See you guys later. Thanks for dinner!"

"Bye!" she calls over her shoulder, too focused on her computer.

Scooting over into Perry's former chair, I look over at the screen. She has several tabs open of different bar websites in the area, reading the 'About Us' pages to see how long each has been in business.

"Any luck?" I ask.

"Not really," she grumbles. "Most of them don't have much information. Who goes on a bar website anyway? Especially the dives, which is more than likely where he'll be. A lot of those don't even have websites, just Facebook pages without very much information."

"What about the ones closest to the warehouse?"

She shakes her head. "They haven't been there long enough. There's one I'm not even sure when it opened."

"Which one?"

Searching through the many tabs open at the top of the browser, she selects one for a bar called "The Scorecard."

"It's right across from the arena," she says. "And only two blocks away from where ESTR used to be."

Looking at the small map in the corner of the page, I note, "Looks like it's right next to a highway."

"Buried highway, but yeah," she says. "But it wasn't always like that. Actually, in 1969 they had just drawn up plans for this route so the area down here would've had a mix of commercial and industrial buildings. The building the Scorecard is in just barely survived, which means he could've went there because it's the only remnant of the area."

Chapter Ten

"Wow, we've really torn down a lot in the last fifty years."

"You have no idea," she says. "Ellsworth is actually not as bad as some cities. Where I'm from in Olympia, there were *a lot* of parking lots until the economy got better. But anyway, yeah, the Scorecard is still there."

"Well, it sounds like a good contender," I say. "Any pictures?"

"Mostly of food," she says. "But they don't list when they opened. Unless…"

"Unless what?"

She opens a new browser and brings up another map. After several more clicks, the screen shows a street view just outside the bar that brings instant recognition to my mind and a bitter taste to my mouth. The tacky vinyl sign above the door shows a baseball glove with the words "The Scorecard" written over it.

"That looks familiar," I say immediately.

"It does?"

"Well, the name doesn't jog any memory and that sign is different, but the building is certainly familiar. Especially that awning." I leave out the part that I distinctly remember throwing up under it the night of my twenty-first birthday. The memory as clear as a bell. Linda patting my back as I hurl, stepping back enough so I don't splatter anything on her shoes.

She changes the street view and the building alters in slight ways with each new image that's loaded. The most notable change is the sign above the door.

"Looks like they've changed names several times over the last ten years. 'The Dugout,' 'Coach's Club,' 'Third Base.'"

My phone dings and I see that I have a new email from Detective Harkness—another thing Perry helped me set up. He's introduced me to the digital world and done his best to help me *not* stand out. I guess getting mad at him for wanting his own place was kind of dumb. Especially when we all knew Rachel wouldn't let me go homeless.

The subject of the email reads "TOP SECRET." Very discreet,

Detective. Opening it, I see images of the switchblade still tucked under the bottom shelf back at the warehouse. The next few images are of the weapon with a bright white background and a ruler beside it. In the email, below the images is a message from her that reads, "You owe me!"

"Do you think this place is a definite contender?" she asks, oblivious to my email.

"Maybe," I say. "Like you said, it's the only surviving building in the area so it makes the most sense. I'll check it out."

"Ash, there could be so many other places he could be," she says.

"We don't have time to scope them all out. I'll see about this place. In the meantime, I need you to do something else for me."

"Like what?"

"I just got pictures of the murder weapon," I tell her. "Could you track that down in a similar fashion to how you tracked down the bar?"

"How the hell am I going to manage that?" she asks.

"See if you can identify the manufacturer or the stores that carry it—which might take you back to 1969. If we can find out where it came from, maybe we can talk to them and see if they've seen Douglas or the Gatekeeper. Hopefully together. That could be another witness for the case against my brother."

She groans. "Tracking down that information could be impossible with my capabilities. Wouldn't you be better off asking someone on Harkness's team?"

"They're probably already be working on it, but I don't want to wait for them. Besides, I don't want to have to go through a mediator every time we need information. Can you please just give it a shot? I'll forward the email to you."

Sighing, she says, "Yeah, I guess I'll see what I can do."

"Thanks." I hit send on the email on my phone and get to my feet. I pull on my gloves and then my mask.

"Where are you going?" she asks.

Chapter Ten

"To the bar to find Donald Douglas."

"Don't you think you should call Detective Harkness for assistance?"

"Why? I can do this on my own."

She shoots me a look. "Besides the *obvious* reason that you could get hurt, calling her will help you mend fences with a very important ally. Don't let your stubbornness get in the way of catching this guy."

Dropping my shoulders, I step toward my phone on the counter again. "I hate it when you make sense."

Chapter Eleven

ASH

"I think this is a waste of time," I say as Detective Harkness and I sit outside the Scorecard in her car. We're watching the front door for Donald Douglas to leave so we can catch him. "Can't we just go in and get him? We don't even know for sure that he's in there."

"We have a pretty good idea that he is, though," she says. "I called into the bar and gave the bartender a description of Douglas. He said he's in there and actually considered throwing him out because of the odor. I told him I'd give him fifty bucks if he let Douglas stay for a bit."

"Yeah, but shouldn't we just go in and grab him? Why give him the opportunity to sneak out the back?"

"Look, we found the murder weapon, right? Which means that he's probably unarmed."

"Not really seeing the problem here," I say.

"Well, just for a moment, I'm jumping into *your* world where it's a real possibility the Gatekeeper has found him and given

Chapter Eleven

him another weapon. Possibly even a gun."

"Even more reason to stop him before he can hurt anyone."

She shakes her head, frustrated. "No! Look, if he has a weapon, we have no idea *what* that weapon is. Not to mention, we don't know where in the bar he is, so it's not like we can sneak up on him. And we know virtually nothing about him so we don't know if surprising him is going to instigate a chase—or worse, a blind shootout."

That logic makes sense but I'm still a little annoyed with the way she flipped out on me back at the warehouse, so I decide not to say anything about her reasoning. Petty, I know, but I still need time before I'm ready to apologize. Maybe even a full night's sleep. Glancing at the middle console, I see it's getting late. Nearly ten o'clock.

"You weren't able to find anything on him?" It's the first time I've been able to really catch up with her on the work she's done today.

"Not anything recent," she says. "We found an arrest report for a Donald Douglas from 1950, which could confirm his story that he's from the 60s, but I can't run with that as part of my investigation."

"No, I guess you can't." Looking out, I watch as the traffic signal at the intersection in front of us changes to green for only one lone car.

"What was the arrest for?"

"Assault," she says. "Got into a bar fight, but it was broken up before any real damage was done."

"Sounds like a match for what you guys picked him up for this morning." My mouth opens into a lion's yawn before I continue. "Even more reason to believe that he's from the 60s."

"Yep. And I had Detective Watkins look into his daughter. He couldn't find anything on her in missing persons, but I found a birth announcement for her from 1951."

"Again, that makes sense with our time travel theory," I add.

"What about Joanie's mother?"

"Died in 1956."

"Joanie was young."

"Yeah. And no other record of her after that. We couldn't verify her employment because City Print Professionals closed in the 80s."

"Okay, so this is all basically confirming that the Gatekeeper is behind this because who else would have the power to do time travel?" I say. "So the question is, how do we find the Gatekeeper?"

"We need to get through to Douglas. Maybe he can help lead us back to the Gatekeeper to save Joanie. I don't want *another* person to die over this stupid sibling rivalry."

"So I take it you haven't been able to locate Arlus Cain either?" I ask, diverting the conversation away from her blaming me and my brother for people dying. I'm aware of it already. I don't need the added guilt while I do what I can to correct it.

She lets out a deep breath. "Not yet. I went to his office and nobody's seen him in a few months, but they said that's sometimes normal because he travels a lot."

"What about his house?"

"Checked that too. His maintenance person let me in."

"And?"

"No sign of Arlus, at least not anytime recent," she explains. "And the maintenance guy said the same thing as the people at his office: it's not unusual for him to jet out unannounced for weeks at a time."

"What about airline tickets? Did you call the airport?"

Harkness nods. "Yep. Nothing. But then—jumping into your world of supers again—if he really can transport himself anywhere, his first mode of transportation would not be one that leaves a paper trail."

"True."

"There's something else, though."

Chapter Eleven

I look over at her.

"At Arlus's house I found the guestbook from your parents' funeral," she starts. "Well, yours too, I suppose."

"Oh."

"Yeah, he had a bunch of old pictures in a cabinet," she says. "I recognized you in some of them."

I look out the opposite window again. I'm annoyed that Arlus has personal mementoes and yet he still insists on waging this war with me. If he cares enough to save old photos, why is he trying so hard to kill me?

"Anyway, the guestbook had an entry in it from Donald Douglas," she continues.

I look back at her quickly. "What?"

"He was at the funeral. He worked with your parents in the mines."

"So that's how he met Arlus."

She nods. "That's what I figured too."

"Interesting."

"Now we know this wasn't random."

"I never thought it was," I tell her. "Too bad it doesn't help us find him. What about his wife or any other family or friends? Would they know where he is?" I think I remember Perry or Rachel mentioning that he was married. And through marriage, he might have additional family.

"*Ex*-wife," she corrects. "And she hasn't seen him in years."

"Do you believe that? She could be covering for him."

"I don't think she is. They've been divorced for almost twenty-five years and she's since remarried. Didn't sound like there was any lingering relationship on any level. No reason for her to lie for him."

"They could've maintained a friendship."

"Not likely. They didn't have a good marriage and she was being very honest about everything."

"I'm just trying to keep the options open," I say.

"Yeah, but sometimes you need to narrow your options so you can focus better. The ex-wife seems like a long shot compared to Douglas, who we *know* has had contact with the Gatekeeper."

"So he's the best bet to finding Arlus and putting an end to all of this."

"Hence why we're sitting out here waiting for him."

The car gets quiet. We both watch out the window at the bar. A group of friends approach the door and enter, smiling and laughing. The light to the left of the door keeps flickering while all the others shine bright. Nothing is particularly out of the ordinary.

The bar is in a weird place. Sure, it's across the street from the stadium, but other than a few empty neighboring storefronts, it's right on the edge of the industrial section of town. At this time of night, it's nearly barren. Makes me wonder how well the bar does year-round. More importantly, it makes me wonder what this place looked like fifty years ago. Besides the memory of me vomiting, nothing vivid is coming to mind about the neighborhood, but that could also be because I rarely ventured down to this end of the city.

I don't really remember this area. Maybe that would change if I actually went into the stadium. Did my parents take me and Arlus to a baseball game when we were younger? Were Arlus and I ever close?

"So what are your plans?" Harkness asks, pulling me out of my thoughts.

"Hopefully Donald Douglas will lead us to Arlus and maybe I can actually get him to talk to me—"

"No, I meant beyond Arlus."

"What do you mean?"

"What are you going to do once Arlus is in custody? With him apprehended, there won't be anymore supers left. The need for Heat won't really exist."

"Let me ask you a question: if you caught one serial killer, would your need at the police department disappear? No, there would still be other murderers."

"We're not just talking about a murderer here, though, we're talking about supers."

"It's the same thing. If Arlus and I both developed powers—and people like Black Magnet and Dust Storm developed powers too—it stands to reason that someone else can develop powers sometime in the future. And they might not decide to do something good with them. And even if that doesn't happen, there will still be murderers and other criminals in the city."

"Yeah, I guess that's true. It makes you wonder, if you said Arlus gave those other people powers, why wouldn't he give Donald Douglas powers?"

"Maybe he did and he just doesn't know it yet. Or maybe Douglas is afraid to use them. Or maybe the Gatekeeper's trying a different approach this time."

"Well, we're going to have to find that out soon."

"The only way to find out is to get him to try to use them," I say. "Not unless Douglas admits it—and he certainly won't tell me."

"I wonder if he hates Heat or just Ash. Both have their own irritating qualities." She looks over at me and smirks.

"Very funny."

"But seriously, what are you going to do long-term? You can't just be Heat all the time. You need to have somewhere to sleep, to eat, to call home. You need a break every once in a while. How can you afford that if you don't have a real job?"

The question of what I'm doing with my life continues to follow me. Maybe it's the universe's sign that I need to seriously think about it and make some changes that'll help me move forward. It's scary to think about because of my continued memory loss. What if it all suddenly comes back to me and I remember the life I have? I know it's dumb to continue to cling to that fantasy, especially with everything that I *have* remembered so far pointing in the direction of me being M.I.A. for fifty years. Yet the hope that I already have an established life here in 2019 still follows me.

"I don't really know," I say truthfully. "A while ago I met someone who knew me back then and she told me I went to school for criminal justice."

Harkness's eyebrows shoot up, along with the corners of her mouth. "Really? That explains how you're crazy enough to be Heat."

"Yeah, yeah."

"Any particular area of criminal justice?"

I motion down to myself, clad in the Heat suit. "Isn't it obvious? I guess it's kind of a second-nature thing. I jumped right into it right after I woke up in the cave."

"Maybe you could join the police academy," she offers. "Of course, you'll probably have to retake your college courses."

"I don't think I really remember them anyway," I add.

"That might not be a bad thing," she says. "Although it would probably blur the line with you being Heat. Of course, if you're a full-fledged police officer, you might not even need to be Heat. You could fight crime the same way the rest of us do."

"Maybe not the *exact* same way." I smirk.

The idea of me becoming a police officer is one I hadn't really considered before. It's been kind of unnecessary because I'm Heat. But Harkness has a point. If Arlus is put away and there aren't any other supers, I could be a cop and still help people, but without the need for my powers. Still, the road to becoming a police officer is daunting.

"This is going to sound weird, but are you…a person?"

I hook an eyebrow, but then straighten my face and say, "You got me. I'm actually an alien from the moon. I escaped here before Apollo 11 could invade my home."

She laughs and adds, "*E.T. phone home!*"

Chapter Eleven

"What was that?"

"That's right, you wouldn't get that. It's a movie from the 80s." She turns to me with wide eyes and says, "Okay history lesson: Do you realize that Apollo 11 actually *did* put men on the moon?"

"On the *moon*?" I ask skeptically. "Are you trying to tell me there's a colony up there now or something?"

Her eyes narrow. "No. They just landed and…collected rocks and stuff, I guess."

"Wait, are you serious?"

She laughs and pulls out her phone. "Yes!" After a few taps and swipes, she pulls up several articles, all celebrating the fiftieth anniversary of the moon landing.

"No kidding," I say, stunned. "They actually landed that hunk of incredibly expensive metal on the moon?"

"You really didn't know? What day did you disappear?"

I shrug. "Whatever day the coal mine explosion was."

She types into her phone again. "That was July 13, 1969. Three days before Apollo 11 launched and a little more than a week before the landing. That was…a long time ago."

"Fifty years," I say. "So wait a minute, we *really* landed on the moon? This isn't a joke?"

"I didn't write all these articles! Look, CNN, the History Channel, *The New York Times*."

"CNN is the news network, right?"

"Oh my gosh, you really have been in a bubble all this time, haven't you?"

"TV is pretty new to me!"

She shakes her head and smiles. "You're something else, Ash."

"Heat," I correct.

"Right, which brings me back to my original question: are you a *legal* person? Like, social security card, photo ID, all of that. Because that's going to need to be straightened out before you even consider any sort of career."

Making a face, I look out to the bar again. No sign of Douglas yet. My doubt that he's even in there creeps up again, along with any thoughts about the alleged moon landing.

"That's what I'm afraid of," I admit. "It's actually a really big deal—or it will be. I can't get a job. I can't buy a car or a house once I have a job. I can't even get married!"

"Are you seeing anyone?" she asks.

"No, but I'd like to eventually, I guess. The person I talked to who knew me then was, uh, my girlfriend. At the time, at least. And one of the reasons I talked to her was because I had a very clear memory of talking to her about our future. We wanted to get married, have a family, but then I disappeared and now here we are."

"I'm sorry." There's not much else she can say.

"What about you?" I ask. "I don't see a ring on your finger."

"No and you probably won't ever, honestly. I'm always working and it's a dangerous job. I can't start a family and ask them to worry about me every day, wondering if I'm going to get hurt. Or worse."

"Right? That's something else I'm worried about."

It feels good to have someone to talk to about this. Someone who isn't as intertwined in my life as Rachel and Perry are. Someone who can offer advice without judgment. Someone who's going through something similar.

"A big reason why I took this job was because it was on the opposite end of the country as the rest of my family," Harkness says. "I didn't want them—my parents, mostly—to have to worry about me every time they watched the evening news."

"I get that." Turning to her, I can't help but chuckle.

"What's so funny?"

"Look at us. We're pretty pathetic, aren't we?"

She smiles and glances back at the bar. "Yeah, I guess so.

Chapter Eleven

Although, *I'm* not as bad as *you*. At least I know that we landed on the moon."

I roll my eyes. "You're not going to let me live that down, are you?"

"It blows my mind that you had no clue!"

"Well, it blows my mind that it happened!"

"True," she says. "I guess the rest of the world has had fifty years to process the enormity of it."

"Anyway," I say, trying to steer us back to the conversation we were having before. "Want some unsolicited advice from someone who isn't any better off than you?"

"I have a feeling you're going to offer it anyway."

"Stop living in fear of what *might* happen and try to go after the things you *do* want," I say. "Life goes on. Priorities change. And if someone really wants to be with you, they'll deal with the madness that is your job."

"Sounds like you should be talking into a mirror."

"Actually no. I'm different."

She rolls her eyes.

"Seriously," I push. "I went on a date with a girl last month simply because she asked me. I didn't go into it with any expectations and just rode it out."

"And?"

"Well…"

"What happened?"

"She sort of ended up in the hospital because Dust Storm attacked her right at the tail end of our date."

"So basically proving my point."

"No, because I did have fun."

"But she got hurt." She adds quickly, "Was this—uh, what was her name?—Melissa?"

I look out my window at the dark entrance for the stadium. "I plead the fifth."

"Interesting. I didn't realize you two were that close."

"Oh, like you've never been interested in someone who was involved in one of your cases," I fire back.

Harkness looks down at her lap. "I, uh, didn't say that."

"Besides, when we went out I didn't know that she was involved in the case at all."

"So what about now that you've broken through your barrier of being afraid? Is there anyone else who you want to test the waters with?"

"Maybe," I say. "But I wouldn't do anything until the threat of the Gatekeeper is gone. Which, at this rate, might never happen."

"There's always going to be another Gatekeeper in this world."

"Is that a quote from a self-help book? Because it's very fitting to real life."

She chuckles. "My point is, you're just going to have to find a way to deal with that and move forward with your life. You should ask this girl out."

"Yeah, but the only problem is—"

She grabs my arm and cuts me off. "There he is."

Through the window, I see a grungy-looking man step through the door and look around outside before turning and disappearing into the darkness of the alley next to the Scorecard.

"That's Douglas," I confirm.

"Let's move."

CHAPTER TWELVE

ASH

Donald Douglas rounds the corner of the Scorecard down an unlit alley.

"Let me try him first," Detective Harkness tells me, but I don't stop as I whip open the car door and soar through the air toward him.

The flames radiating from my body illuminate the dark alley, allowing me to see the terrified expression on Douglas's face as he feebly tries to outrun me.

Big mistake.

The flames cut out in an instant and my momentum carries me forward until I collide with him. He pushes at me, even managing to deliver a solid punch to my rib cage that hurts like hell. Grabbing at his arms, I push him flat on his back onto the pavement and jump on top of him, pinning his arms down with my knees.

"Where's the Gatekeeper?" I bellow.

"Who? I don't know who you're talking about! Somebody

help! Help! This guy is assaulting me!"

It takes all of my energy not to punch him right in the face. Not that it's likely that anyone can hear him from inside the bar with the music playing and the roar of the kitchen vent spewing the scent of greasy food into the alley.

"The man who can open portals," I say. "I know you've seen him. He has a leather mask and—"

"What's going on!?" Harkness rushes up behind me with her gun raised, per her police training. "Get off of him! And can we get some light back here?"

"And let him get away again? I think not."

"Hey, you're that bastard from the warehouse, aren't you?" Douglas asks.

"Hi, Mr. Douglas," she speaks up behind me. "Remember me? I'm Detective Jenna Harkness. We talked this morning. About your daughter? Remember I said I was going to help you before you attacked that man at the station?"

"I didn't attack him!"

"Oh, so spitting in someone's face is a welcome hello in your world?" she asks.

Through the glint of the faint moonlight, I can see him glaring at her.

Undaunted, she presses on, "That warehouse you recognized my friend here from, that wouldn't be the one on West Jefferson Street, would it? Because we found a bloodied knife there that we're confident the DNA will match that of a victim over on Coal Avenue. Being that you were the only one spotted at that warehouse, that would make you a suspect in a murder investigation."

Douglas stammers, but says nothing coherent.

"Seriously, a light?" she snaps at me.

Holding up my left hand, I create a small flame that casts shadows on the brick walls around us. In front of me at the end of the alley sits a dumpster and several overstuffed black garbage bags in front of it. For the first time, I notice the scent of rotting food mixing in with the fryers from inside the kitchen. My stomach churns from the smell, but I keep it down.

"Get off of him," Harkness tells me. "Let him breathe."

Reluctantly, I ease off. He scurries against the dumpster and rises to his feet, but both Harkness and I aim our attacks at him.

"Don't you run away," she tells him. "Your cooperation would be *so gratefully* appreciated."

Slowly, he leans back against the filthy dumpster, but he doesn't seem to care.

"Okay then. Setting the murder aside for now, let's talk about how you got here, Mr. Douglas," Harkness goes on, her gun now pointed in the air, her arms at ninety degrees. "Because last I knew, you were still being held at the police station and I *know* you didn't get authorization to leave. So tell me, how did you get out?"

His eyes dart between me and Harkness until finally he says, "Look, I'm only trying to save my daughter. I didn't mean to do anything—I didn't mean to do any of this."

"Any of what?" she pushes. "What did you do?"

"I didn't—I'm looking for the man from this morning!"

"The man in the mask or the man you spit on?" she asks.

He closes his eyes.

With a sigh, she lowers her gun in an effort to gain his trust. "Look at me, Mr. Douglas." She waits until he slowly turns to her. "Why did you spit on that man you saw at the police station today?"

"What man?"

She raises her eyebrows. "Oh, so you've spat on more than one person today? Don't play dumb, Mr. Douglas. It's in your best interest to tell us the truth."

Again, he looks between us. "Look, I'm just trying to save my daughter. I told you that this morning."

"Joanie," she says.

"Yes. I need to find her."

The fireball in my hand grows slightly larger. "Then *tell us* what you know!"

Harkness puts a hand on my shoulder. "Easy, all right?" Returning to her Good Cop persona, she asks Douglas in a soft voice, "What haven't you told us about her disappearance?"

"I told you everything!"

Slowly, she shakes her head. "I don't believe you did, Mr. Douglas."

More hesitation on his part.

I ask, "Who threatened her?"

"I don't know!"

"Then why are you going after m—*innocent* people?" I stop myself before I ask why he's going after 'me.'

"We found a body today, Mr. Douglas," Harkness goes on, still in her pleasant-but-firm voice. "Not far from where we found you in that warehouse earlier this evening. Being that you're a runaway who was first brought to my attention from an assault claim, I'd say your whereabouts this evening is more than a little suspicious."

"So?" he barks, apparently no longer pacified by her calm demeanor.

"So the victim died of a knife wound and guess what we found in that warehouse you snuck into? Very likely the murder weapon. If the DNA on that weapon matches the DNA of the victim and *your* fingerprints are on it, that's probable cause for arrest. It didn't seem like you planned on killing that man, which makes it at least second-degree murder, which means you're looking at *at least* ten years. And don't think that a maximum security prison will tolerate a little jailbreak like the one you managed today."

Douglas swallows hard. Harkness has his complete attention.

"Now, if you committed this crime because someone is trying

to manipulate you in order to get your daughter back, there's a chance we could work on your sentencing," she continues. "But we're going to need the full story, Mr. Douglas. The *real* story."

"Okay, okay," he stammers, breathless. "The other day, this man came into the office with a mask on. Long coat, boots, really weird. We all assumed he wanted to rob us, which is weird because there's no money in our department."

Sounds like the Gatekeeper to me, but I let him talk.

"Where do you work?" Harkness asks.

That might help us try to figure out what connection he has to Arlus from 1969. Or me.

"In the planning department for the county downtown. An office job."

Doesn't ring a bell.

"Did the man ever reveal himself?" Harkness asks, steering him back on track.

"No."

"Was it normal for people to visit you at work?"

"Not dressed up in masks!" he says. "Occasionally I'd have a meeting with a developer or an executive who was funding a project, but those were always pre-arranged meetings. This guy showed up unexpected and singled *me* out to talk to me."

"What did he want to talk to you about?" she asks.

"Well, he asked to go somewhere private, so I brought him into the empty conference room," Douglas says. "That's when he showed me the picture of my baby girl." He starts choking up.

"What did the picture show, Mr. Douglas?" she asks.

He wipes at his eyes.

She waits another moment and then adds, "I'm sorry. I know this is very difficult to remember, but you need to tell us if we're going to help you."

"My daughter, Joanie, she was…tied up. Tape over her mouth, wrists tied together, makeup smeared. She looked so helpless. She *was* helpless. And he just didn't care."

"Can you remember any details from the picture?" she asks, gentle again. "What was she tied up with? Rope? Electrical cord? Zip-ties?"

"Rope. White rope."

"Just her hands or her legs too?"

He shakes his head. "Couldn't see her legs from the picture."

"Okay, well what about her clothes? Were they new clothes? Were they even *her* clothes? The ones she was wearing the last time you saw her?"

"I don't know," he says. "I didn't pay attention to what she was wearing."

"Were there any distinguishing features in the picture? A mattress, the colors of the walls, maybe a newspaper or something. Did it show anything that might help us determine where she is?"

"There's nothing!" he yells, stepping forward.

I ignite both my fists into flames, which seems to stop him. "Hey! Watch it!"

Harkness holds out her gun with both hands toward Douglas, but by the tone in her voice I can tell she's trying to steady us both. "Okay, okay. Everyone just calm down. Mr. Douglas, there's nothing in that picture that could help us determine where your daughter might be?"

"No, it almost looked like it wasn't real."

Out of the corner of our eyes, Harkness and I exchange glances, immediately jumping on Detective Watkins's theory that this man is crazy.

"The picture was certainly her, but the background was…"

"What was it?" she pushes.

"Um…multi-colored, I guess? It was weird. Not real."

She turns to me to see if I pick up on what he said but I shake my head to tell her it's just as confusing to me.

"Let's go back to the man with the coat," she says. "What did he look like?"

"Leather mask. Thinner. Had a bit of a hunch."

Just like the Gatekeeper. Just like my brother.

"Did he say anything when he showed you the picture?" she asks.

Douglas makes a fist and holds it up to his forehead with his eyes closed. "He asked me if I recognized her. I started asking him where she was, what he did to her, all of it. The bastard smirked. He smiled! That look on his face is never going to leave my mind. He was smug. Knew that he had me in the palm of his hand."

"Any idea why he targeted you?"

He shrugs. "Does it really matter? My daughter's gone. God only knows what he's…" He sucks in a shuddering breath. "I don't know him at all. I don't know why he went after us. Maybe because he knew I was a single father and Joanie would be vulnerable, I don't know."

Vulnerability. That's the common theme running between all of the Gatekeeper's hitmen. Vernon would've faced prison if Arlus didn't make the charges go away. Dr. Isaacs was single and lived alone, so he was an easy target. And now Donald Douglas and his daughter.

"You might not be able to answer this next question, but I want you to think about it: how did you get here, in 2019?" Her gun is still pointed at him.

Douglas lets out a deep breath and looks down. "Back in the conference room, he told me that I would get my daughter back after I did what he asked of me. If I didn't cooperate, both of us would die. Obviously, I agreed, no questions asked. How could I not?"

A part of me wonders if this story is real, especially after Harkness told him that if he tells us everything, she can work with him on his sentencing.

But no, not the way Douglas is acting. This is true worry. Pain. Anger. His emotions are real and they support the reasoning behind his actions. Any father—any *parent*—would do the same for their child.

"Next thing I knew, I was in—this is going to sound weird— but I was in a *different* Ellsworth. This one, I guess. There was a lot that was similar, but also…I don't know—different. This isn't my home." He motions to the bar. "That's about the only thing that looked the same. Figured I could hang out there for a while and find a place to catch some sleep."

"What did the man in the mask ask you to do?" Harkness asks. "In order to get your daughter back."

He tugs at his right ear, fidgeting, buying time before he has to admit to his wrongdoings. Will the threat of harming his daughter be justification enough for a judge to not commit him to a lifetime in prison? I'm too inexperienced with this kind of stuff to even speculate about that and I don't even know the decision I would make if it were up to me.

"That kid I spit on at the police department, the old man showed me his picture and told me I needed to kill him."

"Why?" she asks.

"He didn't say. Just said that he was a very dangerous man who could fool anyone into believing he was on their side," he explains. "Told me not to listen to any of his charms."

Harkness looks over at me and for a fraction of a second, I can see her questioning my loyalty through her eyes. Luckily, that passes quickly. Can't say I really blame her for wondering, though.

"At the time, I didn't even think that guy existed," Douglas goes on, oblivious to our exchange. "Honestly, I didn't really care. I'll do anything to get her back. After I agreed, the man…gave me something. Drugs or something. When I woke up, I thought it was all a dream. Then I saw the tall buildings that aren't in my Ellsworth and I started to panic. That's why I grabbed that woman. It all came flying back to me and my mind just kind of… snapped, I guess. Anyway, when I saw that kid, I knew it all was real and I saw an opportunity to get Joanie back. To save her."

"And you didn't think to tell me this morning about your mission to *kill* a man?"

"Saving Joanie is my top priority!" he shouts. "I thought since I was in the police station that they could help me. That *you* could help me! But instead, you were going to lock me up and treat me like a criminal!"

"So when you saw the man at the station, you thought that was your opportunity to take things into your own hands?"

"Exactly! Then I saw him coming down from the mountain. At least, I *thought* it was him. Looked just like him. Same height, build, all of it. Put up a fight, too, obviously. I—I hated doing it, but the whole time I just thought of how badly I needed to get Joanie back. It didn't hit me what happened until it was over. And he was laying there. And he wasn't even the right kid." He sucks in another shuddering breath. "Oh God, I killed a man!"

"That's why you ran?" I ask. "Because you realized that you committed murder?"

"I didn't—it's not what I *wanted* to do! It's what I *had* to do. I hid out in that warehouse. Found an unlocked door. Figured I could hide out there overnight, but then I heard the sirens. I had to get rid of the murder weapon. I was too disgusted with my-self for what I did, but I still need to get her back!" Tears stream down his face, snot coating his lips, his breath making bubbles between his lips as he talks. "Please! You've gotta help me!"

"Mr. Douglas, I need you to backtrack for a moment," Harkness breaks into his wallowing. "How did you get out of the jail cell?"

He wipes at his mouth and sucks snot up his nose. "He showed up and told me that I was doing a horrible job following through with his orders. Told me again that he was going to kill Joanie if I messed up one more time. This…*thing* opened up—with the colors, like from Joanie's picture—and when I stepped through, I was down here somewhere. Knife in hand, too. A little while later, I saw someone coming down the hill. Someone who looked like that kid—man—from the police station. So I hid in the brush and ran out after him."

"And that's the truth?" she asks him.

"Yes! I'm telling you everything! You said you could help me, right?"

"Well, if we can find this man in the mask and get him to lead us to your daughter, you shouldn't have any trouble—"

Her words are cut off as a giant orb opens in the small space between us and Donald Douglas. The glow from the portal shines immensely brighter than the tiny little flame in my hand does, but only for a moment. Once the Gatekeeper steps out, the orb disperses.

Detective Harkness and I stumble backward, both poised for attack. She doesn't hesitate and fires three rounds directly at the center of the Gatekeeper's chest.

Could it be that simple?

With one swift motion, a small portal opens in front of him and swallows up the bullets. A second later, we hear the load crash as all three drive deep into the side of the dumpster.

Of course it wasn't that easy.

"Run!" Flames shoot out of the palms of my hand toward the newcomer. "Both of you, go!"

My first attack to the Gatekeeper is swallowed up just as Harkness's was, only this time, the flames come right back at me through the second portal, knocking me back into the exterior brick wall of the bar. I crash onto the paved alley and scramble to my feet.

Douglas is on his feet too, inching his way around the Gate-keeper. This alley is a dead end. The only way out is in the Gate-keeper's line of view. I need to distract him so they can escape. Right now, he's too busy watching Detective Harkness. She holds her gun out in front of her, fear disguised by a stern look.

Donald Douglas makes it to the wall of the bar. I put my

hand out to try to tell him to wait, but it's hard to see in the darkness.

"Stand down!" Harkness shouts at my brother. "You're under arrest for—"

The Gatekeeper steps closer and she fires three more times.

Another portal brings light to the alley and sucks up all three bullets before they make contact with the intended target. For a second, we're all painfully quiet until the second portal opens right in front of Douglas, expelling the bullets straight into his chest.

His body convulses with the hits, blood splattering on the wall behind him before he collapses on the ground mere feet away from me.

As quick as I can, I shoot a stream of fire at the Gatekeeper, but he steps through another one of his portals just before the flames reach him. My attack only scorches the side of the neighboring brick building.

"Mr. Douglas, please talk to me," Harkness says in near-hysterics to my left. Her voice is unusually high-pitched. She's crouched over him, her hands on the sides of his face. "Can you hear me?"

Stepping over to her, I watch as she holds her fingers to his throat, checking for a pulse. She looks up at me with a terrified look and shakes her head. "He's dead."

Chapter Thirteen

ASH

Dead?" I ask in disbelief. A minute ago we were just talking to him and now he's gone. Not only that, but it was Detective Harkness's gun that killed him, even if he's not the one she was aiming at. "That's…that's not good."

She stands and brings a shaky hand to her mouth and rests another one on her hip. "No. Not at all."

"What are you going to do?"

"What do you mean, 'what am I going to do?' I'm going to call it in!"

"But that could get you fired, maybe even arrested yourself."

"Ash, this isn't even a question," she says. "I'm the police. I have to call it in. He's a prime suspect in a murder investigation. Someone I said I was following tonight. The fact that he's dead is going to come to light eventually and the bullets they're going to find are mine. The fact that I…" She swallows hard. "The fact that I killed him will be common knowledge before too long anyway. I've worked enough cases to know that the truth always comes out. Better if I just call it in myself and deal with the consequences."

"You didn't mean to do it—" I start, but she cuts me off.

"I know. We both know what happened. But that's not going to bring him back." She pulls out her phone but looks up at me before she calls. "You should get out of here. I don't want to get you in trouble too."

"No, I'm your only witness. The only one who can vouch for the fact that the Gatekeeper is the one who deflected your shot. Not to mention everything Douglas told us before he died. It's not like you got it on record, did you?"

"I didn't know he was going to tell us that. Dammit, I should've taken him back to the station!"

"Where the Gatekeeper would've killed him there," I say. "Douglas said himself that this was his last chance. Us trying to help him get his daughter back got him killed."

"I don't need a guilt trip, Ash!" she shouts, throwing her arms to her side. "I need to protect as many people as I can right now. That means you need to leave."

"I'm not going."

"That wasn't an option. It was an order." Her voice returns to the authoritative tone she uses when she's working.

"I'm not one of your officers," I say. "I don't take orders. So you're either going to call it in now and wait for the rest of the police to show up and question us *both* or we're going to wait until the bar owners find us and a dead body out here on their own. You decide."

Clenching her teeth, she stares at me for a little while longer before pulling out her phone again and dialing. In the silence of the alley, the volume from her speaker is sufficient to hear the ringing sounds pressed up against her ear. When the other end picks up, she jumps right into a nervous spiel.

"Hi, this is Detective Jenna Harkness. Uh…I'm down on Willow Avenue in the alley beside the Scorecard. There's been a, uh…a death. From a shooting."

"Who is the victim?" the male voice on the other end asks calmly.

"A person of interest of ours," she says. "Donald Douglas."

"Does he need medical assistance?"

"No, he's, uh…he's gone."

"You said it was a shooting? Do you know who fired the weapon?"

"Um…" Another hard swallow. "It was my gun, actually. I…I fired."

"Are you alone?"

"No, uh, Heat is here too."

"Heat? The one in the costume?"

"Yeah, the man in the red tights," she says.

Leather, I think, but keep it to myself. Harkness could potentially be marching to her own grave right now. Let them call my suit whatever they want. Of course, it would be nice if they came here knowing, without a doubt, that I'm on their side. But then, even I have to admit that this scene looks *highly* suspicious.

"Okay, a team is already on their way," he tells her through the phone. "Don't go anywhere."

"I'll wait here," she says. "Thanks."

After hanging up, Harkness stands with her back to me still. Her phone is clutched in her hand, which she rests against her lips.

Stepping closer, I gently touch her shoulder. "It'll be okay."

She pulls away and seems to snap out of her funk. "We need to wait on the street. It's not going to help me any if there's a question as to whether we contaminated the crime scene."

"It wasn't a crime."

Stepping back toward the street, she tells me, "That's what they're going to have to treat it as until they can determine that it wasn't. Which might not ever come."

"Don't say that. This wasn't a malicious shoot. You were try-ing to protect Douglas."

"I know what happened, but sometimes that doesn't really matter. Not with these types of cases. All of this *super* stuff com-plicates things. Especially in a system that isn't designed to ac-commodate for the supernatural. I'm screwed."

I reach over and hook my arm around her and she leans into it. When we reach the light from the city street she pulls away and brings back her façade of serious policewoman.

We only have to wait a few minutes before the first police-men arrive. The flashing lights from atop of their cars takes care of the dark alley problem, but they still set up portable flood lights at the back of the alley to brighten up the space. Harkness steps into the alley to point out clues while I stand aside, catch-ing nervous and confused glances as more police personnel ar-rive. It isn't until I see Detective Watkins pull up that I decide to follow Detective Harkness to the back of the alley.

"Jenna, what the hell is going on?" Watkins fumbles with his latex gloves, struggling to put them on over his chubby, hairy fingers. "You *shot* someone?"

"It's a long story, Walt." No sign of malice in her voice this time. She's talking to him as a friend, which she desperately needs right now.

"Give me the quick version so I know what I'm going into." He studies her, worry in his eyes.

Harkness stares at the CSI team swarming around Donald Douglas's body. They search the area, quickly noting the blood splatter on the wall and even find the bullets lodged into the side of the dumpster.

"Six shots total," one of them tells Watkins. "Three in the victim. Through and through. Ballistics will have to confirm, but the bullets look like they could be .40 S&W."

With wide eyes, Watkins turns back to Harkness. "What the hell happened here?"

"For the sake of your own job, Detective, I suggest you go by the book with this one," she says. "Treat me as if I'm anyone else, unless you'd rather excuse yourself from the case."

"Jenna, this isn't just any other case—"

"You don't know that for sure yet," she cuts him off. "As I said, you need to just do your job or find another detective to take the case."

He looks between me and her for a moment and then sighs heavily, pulling out his notepad. "What's with him?"

Glancing up at me, she mutters, "He was here when it happened."

An eyebrow goes up on Watkins's wrinkled face.

"Detective Harkness was trying to protect Donald Douglas," I say.

"Okay, you go stand over there." He waves his notepad at me and motions to the other side of the alley. "I'll talk to her first and decide what's going to happen from there."

Stepping back to where he pointed, I try to stay out of the way as CSI does their job. The flood lights they've set up makes the area look like a completely different reality than what I remember. Harkness, Douglas, and I were just talking. Sure, it started as a sort of manhunt, but he was giving us answers. Telling us what we needed to hear to help him and his daughter.

Which is why the Gatekeeper showed up to kill him.

Can he hear us from anywhere? Did he plant a bug on Douglas? The police will find that when they take Douglas's body in. Either way, it's scary to think that the Gatekeeper might be listening in at any moment. It also begs the question: why has he only attacked me at selective times if he can listen in to any conversation?

After a few more minutes, Detective Harkness disappears down the alley toward the street and Detective Watkins approaches me.

"So, Superman," he starts.

"*Heat.*"

He looks at me over his notepad and scrawls down my name. "No chance I can get you to take the mask off, is there?"

"No, sir."

He sighs again. Or maybe he's just a loud breather. That could be it too. "All right, why don't you tell me what happened?"

I dive into a brief story about how I figured out where Donald Douglas might be hiding out—leaving out Rachel's name and saying I simply followed the story Douglas was telling us—and called Harkness to check it out. How we waited until Douglas walked out before approaching him and how he told us more about what happened with his daughter, adding that it was all non-violent until the Gatekeeper showed up.

That brings a disbelieving look from Detective Watkins, but he doesn't stop me. He lets me tell him how we fired at the Gatekeeper, Detective Harkness following protocol the entire time, but his powers redirected her shots to Donald Douglas.

"And he just disappeared?" Watkins asks at the end of my story.

"Yeah. He hired Douglas to do a job and Douglas failed so he killed him."

Folding up his notepad, Watkins tucks it into his back pocket. "Well, if you two are lying, you've come up with a very detailed story. Lucky for you, I believe my partner."

"What's going to happen to her?"

"I really don't know yet." He looks back at the rest of the police crew. "Internal affairs will take over the investigation. They'll determine the nature of the shooting and what kind of disciplinary action might need to be issued."

"She really was only trying to help. She didn't mean to kill him."

Another heavy breath. Must be that's just the way he breathes. "I know, but I need to look at the facts here as well as I can under the law. There aren't any rules for how to deal with supers like yourself. So this Gateman—"

"Gatekeeper."

"Whatever. Him showing up needs to be taken as another person present at the scene, but I can't consider the fact that he has super abilities. That's not going to hold up in court if we make an arrest based off that assumption. And even if we did, we wouldn't be able to contain him."

I nod. "Yeah, hopefully that'll change soon, though." Perry better come through with a design for a super prison cell. With each passing moment, the need for it increases.

"As much as I hate it, my hands are tied."

"So she could get in trouble for this? Even though it was am clean shoot?"

"Well, you and her were the only ones present to say it was a clean shoot. And a suspect is very likely going to lie to protect themselves, which, unfortunately, Harkness is the suspect in this situation. As for you, we'd first need to confirm your statement. And second, even if we did, as long as you're hiding behind that mask, your statement doesn't mean anything because we can't prove that Heat is always the same person. Anyone can put on your suit and claim to be you."

"But they can't," I argue. "Nobody else has these powers like I do."

"Maybe so, but unless you're willing to reveal your identity, there's nothing else I can do. I'm sorry. I wish I could count on your statement, but I very much doubt internal affairs will take what you say seriously."

"Even with all I've done to help the city?"

"I'm not denying what you've done. I'm just telling you the way it is. I'm sorry. Trust me, I don't want to see anything bad happen to her, either. I'll do what I can to protect her. In the meantime, you should get going. I should be arresting you right now, but if Harkness trusts you, then I'm going to believe in her." Watkins offers a crooked smile and turns back into the alley.

Chapter Thirteen

I watch as he walks off to join the CSI team. Hoping that Harkness is still here, I head out to the street and find her leaning against her car, watching the police lights flash at the end of the alley.

"How are you doing?" I ask her.

"As good as I can, I guess. You didn't get in trouble for anything, did you?"

"No." I lean next to her against the car and cross my arms. "I wasn't the one who fired and Douglas doesn't have any burns on him, so…"

"Right. Yeah."

"I did everything I could to try to convince him you're innocent," I tell her.

"I know. And I know Watkins believes us, but there's only so much he can do if he wants to keep his job."

"Yeah, it still stinks."

Turning to her car now, she says, "I should probably head home. No sense in me being here anymore."

"What did they tell you?"

She rests her hands on her hips inside her jacket and reveals an empty gun holster.

Noticing my gaze, she drops her arms and tells me, "They have me on administrative leave until internal affairs can come to a conclusion."

"You lost your job?"

"Right now it's only temporary."

"But who's going to lead the investigation into Arlus?"

"All of my cases will be passed on to Detective Watkins," she says. "He's my partner and has been working on them with me the whole time."

"But he doesn't know everything about the Gatekeeper, or what we just heard. It could be weeks before he does something and by then—"

"I don't know," she cuts me off.

"Things aren't exactly stacked in your favor, are they?" I ask.

"No. And the extra bullets in the side of the dumpster suggest that I was chasing him."

"If only they could take my statement. Maybe that would be enough to exonerate you."

"I doubt that alone would make the difference, but maybe," she says. "Getting the Gatekeeper arrested is the only surefire way that I'll get out of this untouched. Even then, if he doesn't confess to redirecting my shot, I could be screwed either way. Short of them accepting your testimony, my leave could be indefinite."

CHAPTER FOURTEEN

ASH

"You don't have to walk me inside." Detective Harkness stands outside the door to her apartment. It's a duplex just south of downtown. Only a few streets over from where Vernon's house was. I wonder how his family is holding up.

"It's late," I tell her, still in my Heat suit. All of my other clothes are back at Rachel's.

"Yeah and I've been a cop long enough to know how to handle myself."

"Without your gun?"

"I have my baton."

"Oh, right. Your gun didn't work against the Gatekeeper but a stick will."

She rolls her eyes before glancing to the door. The building looks like it was once ornately decorated but has since been whitewashed with builder-grade "improvements." The front door retains its tall glass panels, but the original woodwork has been sloppily painted white. It's not the only house in the area that's had a similar remodel. Despite only being a couple streets over from the stately mansions on South Center Street, this neighborhood is quite different. The lack of street trees doesn't help any.

"You're not going to let me go inside by myself, are you?"

"No, ma'am."

She hooks an eyebrow. "First of all, don't call me that. It makes me sound old. And second, I'm only giving in to this 'hero' thing you've got going on right now because I've had a long day and I don't have the energy to argue." With that, she turns her key in the lock and opens the door.

Inside, the décor helps distract from the hasty maintenance decisions of her landlord. We step into a narrow hallway with a cased opening leading right to her living room. A crème afghan is tossed on the loveseat against the far wall, which is pointed to the TV in the corner. On the floor lays a gray and white ornamental rug with an antique leather trunk sitting on top as a makeshift coffee table. Next to the window sits a short bookcase filled with worn paperbacks on its shelves and several scented candles on top.

"Sorry about the mess." Harkness hangs her purse on the coat hook by the door and steps into the living room to fold up the blanket and grab a few errant dishes.

"Didn't even notice." I nod to the curtains hooked to the sides of the windows. "You mind pulling those?"

Setting the folded blanket on the couch, she moves over to the windows and pulls the curtains shut, flicking the switch on the standing lamp in the corner as she passes.

"Go on." She motions to the rest of the house. "Inspect."

I step through each room, just to make sure it's clear. The Gatekeeper probably would only show up when Detective Harkness is alone, so checking the house is kind of pointless. Except, a nagging worry in the back of my head tells me that he could've easily pulled someone else from the street—maybe even anywhere in time, really—and given them the same task as Donald Douglas.

After checking the whole house, I meet her in the kitchen. It's small with cracked tiled flooring and plywood cabinets. Nothing spectacular, which is surprising to me. Maybe the original kitchen is on the other side and this was the hasty addition.

"It's all clear," I announce.

"Good. Why don't you take off that mask and sit for a minute?" The microwave beeps and she steps toward it with a set of potholders. "Did you even have anything to eat tonight?"

I pull off my mask and run my hands through my matted hair. "I did, actually, but with everything that's happened I don't think I'd turn down another meal."

"Go take a seat in the living room and I'll bring something over," she says. "I hope you don't mind reheated pasta."

With no other seating options, I plop down on one end of the loveseat and try not to think about how uncomfortable this Heat suit is in a seat like this. I'm not used to sitting in it. Today in Harkness's car was probably the longest I've ever sat with it on. Perry designed it to chase after criminals and withstand infernos, not to lounge on a couch.

She comes out a minute later, balancing a bowl in each oven mitt-covered hand.

"Careful, it's hot," she tells me as she sets it down on the old trunk.

Inching up to the edge of the seat, I lean over and blow into the bowl.

Harkness sits beside me and does the same. "I have to be honest with you. It's actually nice to have some company for a change." She checks the time on her phone. "And midnight is about right for a police detective—well, *former* police detective."

"Hey, don't talk like that," I say between bites. "You don't know what's going to happen. Just take the rest of tonight to not think about it and tomorrow you can dive in to your plan to move forward."

"If I can come up with one."

"Nope. That's tomorrow's problem. The only thing you should be thinking about right now is if you've had enough to eat."

"Hardly." She scoops another bite into her mouth and chews for a minute. "Remembering to eat when I'm working a case is a real struggle of mine."

"This is good. What is it?"

Her eyes quickly dart back to her food before she looks at me with skepticism. "Pasta-Roni?"

"Is it like Noodle-Roni?"

She blinks at me. "Isn't that the same thing?"

"Is it?" I shrug. "I've been living under a rock, so the hell if I know." Probably another cultural reference that's lost on me, just like the moon landing.

She smirks. "You're interesting."

"Interesting how?" I ask before taking another bite.

"Well, first of all, you're from the *past*, second, you *throw fire*, and third, even though you don't know who exactly you are, you're still passionate about making sure everyone else is doing okay. That's…pretty amazing."

"Meh, I look at it like this: my life is basically non-existent here, so I have nothing to lose and everything to offer. Why wouldn't I do what I can to help?"

She smiles and taps my knee. "That's a great outlook on life."

"I'm wise for my seventy-two years." I laugh.

"Seventy-two? Oh, I guess—wait, you're only twenty-two?"

"According to my girlfriend from my past, I was twenty-two when I disappeared and Perr—my friends guessed that I didn't age in those fifty years."

"Perry?" She taps her fork against the edge of her bowl. Both of ours are nearly halfway empty and at least for me, my stomach is second guessing having another meal tonight.

I push my bowl away and lean back on the couch. "Yeah."

"I met him at EIT during all of that business with Dust Storm."

"Right, yeah."

"Don't worry. His secret is safe with me," she says. "Especially now that I'm—"

"Hey, we're not talking about that tonight."

"Right, sorry." She stabs her fork in what's left of her bowl and sets it on the trunk. A moment later, she leans back beside me, our shoulders leaning against each other.

"You're going to be okay," I assure her. "You were doing the right thing. So even if they can't see that, the universe will reward you later on."

"I thought we weren't going to talk about it?"

"One last comment can't hurt."

She smiles again. "Well thanks. And for the record, I think you can create a life in this time period. You're just going to need to take off the mask now and then. Heat might be an incredible asset to this city, but Ash Cain is a very good person too."

"You barely know Ash Cain."

"You could show me."

I raise my eyebrows. "What are you suggesting?"

She studies me, her eyes glancing down at my lips briefly just before she leans forward and kisses me.

Just as quickly as it happens, it's over.

"What was that?" I smile without thinking.

"A thank you," she says. "For being here for me. And a risk I decided to take based off our conversation in the car earlier."

I stare at her, still in shock of what just happened, trying to figure out the best path forward.

"Detective Harkness—"

She scoffs. "We just kissed. I think you can call me Jenna.

But only when I don't have to call you Heat."

I sigh and pull away from her. "I don't think this is a good idea."

"Oh. Right." She sits up and stacks our bowls on top of each other, rising to her feet. "I'm sorry. I'll just—"

I get up and follow her to the kitchen. "I don't want to ruin our working relationship. We're still figuring things out, but we're doing okay in that department."

Standing over the garbage, she scoops the leftovers in the trash. "That makes perfect sense."

Her inability to meet my eyes says otherwise.

"Jenna—"

"Actually, I think you should probably stick with Detective Harkness. Wouldn't want to interfere with anything."

"I didn't mean to hurt you," I say. "It's not that I didn't like the kiss. I just think that right now the two of us—"

"The two of us *what*?" She leans against the counter, one hand on her hip, and stares at me with her head cocked. "That we're not in a place to be with anyone right now? Then what was all that stuff about in the car? 'Stop living in fear of what might happen. If someone really wants to be with you, they'll make an effort.'"

"Jenna," I say, refusing to revert back to her more formal name. "I meant what I said, but I also said that things for me are really complicated right now. And if you get involved with someone who doesn't *legally* exist, it's going to raise suspicions at the police department. This is the last thing you need right now."

She scoffs again and carries the bowls to the sink. "You're just watching out for me, is that it?"

"Yes!"

Ignoring me, she scrubs the bowls under the water with a sponge. "Well, I think you're right about one thing. This day is in desperate need of ending. Just go home—or wherever you're staying—and we'll talk in the morning when we've both had some rest, okay?"

I eye up the door before looking back at her. She places the bowls on a towel beside the sink and leans on her soapy hands on the edge of the counter with her eyes closed.

"I'm sorry."

"Don't be." She wipes her hands and lets out a heavy sigh. "You're not exactly wrong. I guess I'm just not in the right headspace right now. It's been a long, *horrible* day. We'll figure it out in the morning. Just go."

"If you need anything through the night—"

"I'll call you, yes."

"Okay, well, I guess I'll see you tomorrow then." I grab my mask from the living room and slide it on.

"Ash!" She hurries over to me before I exit.

"Yeah?"

"Thanks for coming home with me. It was a rough day."

"Of course, yeah. I'll see you tomorrow." I offer her a smile and slip through the door.

———

"SO DETECTIVE HARKNESS is suspended?" Rachel asks over breakfast the next morning.

"Administrative leave," I correct. "But yeah, she's not reporting for work and she's definitely off the Joanie Douglas case *and* the Peter Jones case."

"Well, the prime suspect in the Peter Jones case is dead."

"Yeah, and that's going to come back to bite us all in the ass." I take another stab of my eggs. "These are delicious, by the way."

"Thanks," she murmurs. "I added pepper. Nothing too special."

"It's good."

"It's a shame, though."

"That I like the eggs?"

"No, that Donald Douglas is dead."

"Oh," I say. "Yeah. I feel really bad about it. He confided in us because he finally understood that we were trying to help him. Too bad my brother's just a jerk."

"Worse than a jerk," she adds. "But that's not what I was talking about. While you were out dealing with everything that happened between Harkness and Douglas, I was looking into that switchblade. The one they suspected Douglas used on Peter Jones?"

"He confessed to it last night, but that might not mean anything with the way things are now."

"We'll have to wait and see."

"Did you find where he got the knife?" I ask.

"It took some work, but I think so. I had to track down the manufacturer, luckily got someone on the phone last night who gave me a list of what stores sold the blade in Ellsworth. I gave her some story about my grandfather purchasing it for my father back in the 60s and that I wanted to track down the particular store. She dug around and found a partial list of the Ellsworth stores that carried it back then. Before the computer age, record keeping wasn't as in-depth."

"Only a partial list?"

"Luckily a partial was all I needed. I think. I tracked it down to a place on Willow Avenue that's still open. Sansone's Sporting Goods. Honestly, it probably hasn't changed much since the 60s. And I'm guessing that's why Douglas went there."

I shake my head. "He told us last night that when Arlus sprung him from jail, he *just happened to have* the knife."

"Liar."

"Maybe, but either way, I don't think Douglas is the one who purchased the blade."

"Okay..." She considers for a while. "Well, we already

assumed that Arlus was testing out his powers these last few months, right?"

"Possibly, yeah."

"So maybe he went back to the 60s to try to stop the coal mine from exploding—although that would create an infinite loop because without the fire in the coal mine, Arlus wouldn't have gotten his powers, which would prevent him from coming back to stop the fire to begin with and if he didn't come back to stop the fire, then the fire would still happen and—"

"Rach, you're losing me."

"Sorry. My point is, maybe Arlus went back to 1969 and once he realized he couldn't stop the fire, he came up with a new plan."

"Kidnapping Douglas's daughter?"

She nods. "And having Douglas kill you. If he didn't have access to the coal mine—or didn't want to mess up the time-line—then maybe that's why he's relying on Douglas to kill you without any powers."

"So he purchased him a knife," I add, catching on to where her theory is going.

"Uh-huh. And since the 2019 Arlus went back to 1969, he went to the only sporting goods store he could think of to purchase a knife like that."

"Sansone's."

"There was no Wal-Mart back then."

"Wal-Mart?"

"Never mind," she says. "Either way, Arlus must've gotten the knife and given it to Douglas to kill you."

"Wouldn't Arlus want to keep his prints off of the blade?" I ask.

"He could've worn gloves."

"Walked into a store with gloves on and purchased a weapon? That's suspicious, even for 1969."

"Well then maybe he cleaned them," she says. "Do you know for sure it was only Douglas's prints on the knife?"

"No. The crime lab still had it when everything happened with Harkness."

"Well, the bottom line is, the best I could find on the knife's origins is Sansone's on Willow. All we can do is go there and ask about Douglas or Arlus. But if he bought it in 1969, it's going to be a stretch."

"Still worth a shot." I pop the last bite of my eggs in my mouth and murmur around them, "I'll go."

"Not alone."

"I can't ask Harkness to continue to investigate this case while she's on leave," I tell her. "That's only going to get her in further trouble. And I'm not going to put you or Perry at risk. I need to go in as Heat and I don't want either of you two connected with him to protect your own identity. I'll put a comm on and you guys can be in my ear the whole time. Speaking of, have you heard from Perry?"

She shakes her head. "I was going to ask you. I wonder how much he really got done on that super prison cell last night."

"If he went in at all," I say. "Maybe Violet got out of work early and he skipped out."

"I don't think he'd do that," she says. "He knows how important this is and he promised you he'd do it. He's still your friend and he's working hard to give you what you need to close this case."

"Yeah, I guess you're right. Still kind of bitter that I needed to leave."

She rolls her eyes. "As if his couch is *so much better* than the queen-size bed in my spare bedroom here. Ash, get over it. Things change and you actually got a better deal this way."

I smile, glad that she called me out on my whining. "Okay, you're right. I'm going to go get changed and then head down to the shop. I want to be there when they open. I don't want any customers getting in the way of me questioning the owners."

Chapter Fifteen

Detective Harkness

The phone cuts to voicemail again. Third time now. Jenna Harkness gets an uneasy feeling in the pit of her stomach. What if something happened to him?

She carries her cup of coffee to the living room and sets it on the trunk coffee table. She stares at the sun gleaming through the window—the first time in a long while she's seen her living room in this light. Meanwhile, she tries not to panic as she sits here, unable to do anything to stop a killer or get in touch with the one person who could otherwise stop him.

Administrative leave is a drag.

Grabbing the remote, she clicks on the TV as a distraction. When was the last time she got to watch TV at this hour of the morning? Or any time of day, really. The morning talk shows bring back a sense of nostalgia for her from when she was a little girl growing up. Summer mornings spent lazily watching TV until her mother urged her to get outside and play.

Despite the memories, her mind still wanders to Ash. Maybe

it's still too early for him. They were up late last night and he could still be sleeping.

Dialing his number again, she murmurs to herself as it rings, "Come on, Heat. Pick up."

Harkness had woken up to a call from internal affairs earlier this morning, asking to get in touch with Heat. Said they needed to ask him some more questions about the shooting last night.

Maybe that's why he isn't answering. He's scared that this might come back on him.

Or it could be that she really freaked him out when she kissed him. It felt natural at the time but even now she regrets doing it. And he was right to put an end to it. She wouldn't go around kissing Detective Watkins—besides the fact that he's married—so why would Heat be any different? They're colleagues, no matter how intimate the moment felt at the time.

Back to voicemail. Harkness ends the call and tosses her phone on the other end of the couch. She picks up her coffee and cradles it in her hands, blowing on it before taking a careful first sip.

Who would know where Ash is? He said he has friends but at the moment, she can't remember their names. He was very careful not to bring them up in front of her to protect them. Hopefully that doesn't wind up to be his fatal mistake.

After all he's faced so far, she doesn't want to see him get hurt. For once, she's actually in the same shoes as her family is with her. Watching the news, worrying, wondering if the next criminal is going to be the one to take her life.

Ash is different, though. His powers give him a strength she doesn't have. They also bring enemies that she wouldn't normally face, either. If it wasn't for him, Dust Storm would've—

Dust Storm.

EIT.

Perry.

Springing to her feet, spilling some hot coffee on her hands,

Harkness rushes up the stairs to change. She might not know where Ash is, but she knows someone who might be able to find him.

———

"AM I IN trouble or something?" Perry asks once he and Harkness are in the basement lounge outside his office. It's not exactly private—not with two students working at opposite ends of the room with headphones in—but it's the best she could do.

"No, nothing like that," she says. "I was actually wondering when the last time was that you heard from Ash?"

"Yesterday, why? Is *he* in trouble?"

"Not with the police."

His eyes grow wide. "With…?"

"Possibly," she says. "Do you have any way of getting in touch with him?"

He pulls out his phone. "I could try calling him."

"I tried that."

Perry dials anyway, bringing the phone to his ear and staring at his shoes as it rings and rings. "He's not answering."

"I know. I tried a few times this morning." At least now she knows Ash isn't just ignoring her.

Pulling the phone away from his ear, he ends the call and taps the screen several times. "His, uh, *Heat tracker*," he whispers, "isn't showing anything. But that could just mean that he doesn't have the suit on."

"What difference does that make?"

"I designed it to only kick on when it registers his body heat. So it only works when he wears it."

"And it's not showing him anywhere on there?" she asks.

"No."

"Does it show his last location?"

He shakes his head. "It's not showing anything, but let me

see if I can pull it up on my computer. The capabilities of the app aren't as advanced as the program on my desktop."

"All right, let's go then."

Perry leads her back into his lab. She stands in front of his desk as he clicks around on his computer. His coworkers in the room pretend not to notice her, but she catches a few traveling glances her way. They must remember when she arrested one of their other coworkers. His empty desk still sits beside Perry's.

"Huh." He stares at his computer screen.

"Did you find him?" she asks.

"His last location is some place on Willow Avenue."

"Which part?"

"Between Sixth and Seventh Streets."

"The commercial district?" she asks. "That could be a million places."

"It's not giving any more of an exact location than that," he says. "The storefronts are all too small to indicate which one he was at."

"How long ago was that?"

"An hour ago," he says. "Let me try calling Rachel."

"Is she your other friend?"

Perry looks up at her with a hint of panic in his eyes. "Uh… yeah, she is. Ash has been staying with her." He pulls his phone up to his ear and gets to his feet, leading them back out to the lounge. "Hey, have you seen Ash?" He waits, then says, "No, it's just that Detective Harkness hasn't heard from him and I can't get in touch with him." Another pause, then, "Yeah, I saw that he was on Willow Ave. What's he doing there?" Perry looks up at Harkness as he listens. "A sporting goods store? Oh, from the murder?"

Harkness pulls out her phone and does a quick Google search for any sporting goods stores on Willow Avenue. There used to be a ton of them in the city back when so many people fished out of the Percival River. Thanks to urbanization, only one store survives at 549 Willow Avenue: Sansone's Sporting Goods.

Without waiting for Perry, she turns to the stairs and starts walking up.

"Yeah, thanks Rach," he says quickly, then calls to her, "Where are you going?"

One of the students in the lounge looks up at them before returning to their work.

"I'm going to find Ash."

"I'm coming with you."

"The hell you are," she says. "You don't know what you could be walking into."

"Neither do you," he pushes. "And Rachel told me that as of right now, you're not even supposed to be doing any police work."

That stops Harkness in her tracks. How many people knew about that already? It happened less than twelve hours ago.

"Look, I might not be a cop and neither of us are supers, but I know more about them than you do," he says. "Let me help."

She studies him for a while, doing her best to determine how dangerous of a situation this might be. There's no way to tell. And without her weapon to protect her, she can use all the backup she can get.

"Okay fine. But do as I say."

"Yes, ma'am."

"Don't call me that!"

———

"YOU SURE IT'S not a problem that you left work early?" Harkness asks Perry as she pulls out of the Ellsworth Institute of Technology campus.

"I worked late last night, so I have some time." He looks down at his phone. "Go right at the next light, that'll take you down Willow."

"I know. I've driven around this city a few times."

"Oh right. Sorry."

"It's fine. I will need help finding where exactly Sansone's is," she says, throwing him a bone.

"I can help with that."

The two of them are quiet as they sit at the intersection, waiting for the light. Despite the sun, there's a chill in the October air so the windows are closed, making the awkward silence even more prominent.

"So what is it you do at EIT?" she asks.

"Technology Development Engineer is my official title," he says. "Basically, I invent stuff."

"Anything cool?"

"Actually, Ash has had me pretty busy lately."

"He pays you?"

"Are you kidding?" He chuckles. "Ash doesn't have any money! No, I work on devices that'll help him. Write up the schematics and submit them to the school as my own inventions. The school gets to claim the tech so they're happy and Ash gets to use the tech so he's happy. It's a win-win."

"Like the tracer?"

"Yeah, except I've been dragging my feet on bringing that one to the school," he says. "Trying to think of the best way to spin it so it doesn't sound as creepy as it is."

She laughs. "Say it's for police work. I could've used something like that on a suspect yesterday. Course there's the legalities of it to consider, but it would've made things easier."

"Donald Douglas?"

The light changes and she hits the accelerator a little too eagerly. "Yeah, him."

"Did you get him?"

Flicking on her signal, she moves into the turning lane and waits for the lights to change again. "I'd rather not talk about that right now. Why don't you tell me about some of the stuff you came up with for Ash?"

"Well, last night I finished up work on what I've been calling a Vision Viewer."

"And that would be...?"

"A way for Ash to re-experience some of his flashbacks to help him pick up on minor details he missed the first time," he explains. "I figured it'd help him remember more of his past."

"That sounds cool. How would you pass that off to the college, though?"

"Dream studies," he says. "That's essentially what his visions are anyway."

"Do you think it'll work?"

"I hope so," he says. "Ash is kind of my guinea pig, to be honest. But he doesn't seem to mind."

She smiles and follows the car in front of her onto Willow Avenue. Like it is every day, the street is a madhouse to drive down. Small storefronts line both sides of the street, each offering something unique and quirky. Restaurants, bakeries, and small cafés are interspersed throughout the street, providing sidewalk seating and further crowding the strip.

Willow Avenue is great from an economic standpoint, but horrible from a policing standpoint. Traffic is a nightmare as people struggle to parallel park on the street, causing a traffic jam with the drivers who expect to fly down the straightaway. And that's not counting the small, historic storefronts that aren't all equipped with the same level of security as new builds.

"With Ash being M.I.A. I'm kind of kicking myself now for devoting time to the Vision Viewer last night instead of something more useful," Perry says just before Harkness hits the brakes to avoid hitting a car that shoots out quickly from its parking space on the street.

She groans at the car, but softens her voice when she says, "You couldn't have known he would disappear."

"No, but I could've worked on the actual project he told me to."

"Which was?"

"A prison cell that would dampen the powers of supers."

"Oh," she says pointedly. "Yeah, we could really use something like that."

"You don't have anyone developing that for you?" he asks.

"That would require the department to recognize that these supers aren't going away," she says. "Besides, whenever you're spending taxpayer money, everything moves at a snail's pace. Having someone come to us who already has the technology available would mean that our prisons are more equipped sooner. If you ever work out all the kinks and you're the first one to do it, it could be really big for you and the college."

"I didn't think about that."

"Not to put any pressure on you." She inches forward and stares at the license plate in front of her. PLE-4365. If this guy does anything illegal, his license number will be etched into her brain with how long she's been sitting behind him.

"Well, now that Ash has gone and walked right into a trap—"

"We don't know for sure that it's a trap," she corrects.

"Either way, being unable to find him is a reminder that the power dampener should've been top priority."

"You can make it top priority now."

"Doesn't help Ash in the meantime," he says.

"But it will once we find him. And I think it's a really good idea if you can develop it because right now, even if we catch the Gatekeeper—who is very likely behind all of this—we have no way to contain him. So whether or not we get lucky and get him at a moment of weakness, if we can't keep him in a prison cell like all the other criminals, he still wins."

Chapter Sixteen

ASH

My head is pounding. My eyes are heavy. My body feels weak.

What happened? Last thing I remember I was walking up to Sansone's Sporting Goods in my Heat suit, about to grab the door and then—nothing. It's completely wiped from my memory.

Desperately, I scramble in my head to see if I've lost anything else. My name is Ash. I was born in 1947. Disappeared in 1969. Woke up again in 2019.

With the highlights having been acknowledged, I move on to more pressing concerns: where am I and how did I get here?

My eyelids are still too heavy to open, so I focus on other senses. I'm lying down. Moving my hand, I try to determine what it is I'm lying on—noting that I'm still wearing my Heat suit. I can't figure out what it is I'm on. It's firm, but still pliable.

The Gatekeeper

Sucking in a deep breath, I struggle to sit up, but I manage. Slowly, I open my eyes and blink several times, trying my best to focus them.

I'm not in a room or any type of man-made structure. Yet this certainly isn't nature. Definitely not anything that can be found in Ellsworth. The walls seem endless, yet measurable. Almost like a bubble, only whatever's on the outside can't be seen. Not with the swatches of colors splattered along the mysterious walls—and *moving*. Blues, mostly, mixed in with shades of greens and purples too.

What the hell is this place?

To my right, I notice someone else lying on their side, facing the other way. A girl. Her tangled blonde hair prevents me from determining whether or not she's hurt—or dead. She's in a powder blue skirt, but is barefoot.

But what is she doing here? Wherever *here* is. How did she get mixed up in—

My memory starts to clear. This must be Joanie. Donald Douglas's daughter. The girl we've been trying to find.

Instantly, regret fills me that I found her less than twelve hours after Douglas was killed.

"Hello, brother."

The voice immediately pulls my attention away from Joanie. My head rocks back and forth but I can't place where the sound is coming from. Where is he?

It takes an enormous amount of strength to rise to my feet. My head feels heavy, but I muster through it. I need to be on full alert right now.

"Where are you?" I ask, continuously turning around. If whatever the Gatekeeper gave me that made me groggy doesn't give me a headache, all this spinning will.

"Here." He pops up a few feet in front of me, a safe distance away from Joanie.

I run to him, but the space between us doesn't change. The

next instant, he's gone.

"There," he says from beside me, right next to Joanie.

Whipping around, I catch sight of him but he disappears again.

"Everywhere." His voice booms loudly from above. "You see, brother, this is my own world. I'm in complete control here."

I try to erupt into flames, but the level of heat I'm able to attain stifles out almost immediately.

"I wouldn't rely too much on that," his voice says from… somewhere. "In this world of mine, I get to influence the out-side elements that might have…consequential effects on your firepowers."

"What do you want?" I bellow up above me. "Why did you trap us here?"

"Well, you've finally found the girl," he sneers. "It's a shame. I didn't want to hurt her, but you were leaving me with very little options."

"You killed her?" I look over at her, searching to see if she's breathing, but with her back to me I can't make it out.

"No, she's alive. I've just given her a few sedatives to keep her…cooperative."

"She has nothing to do with this! This is between you and me."

"Right you are, but we're not little kids anymore, Ashton. And now that we're adults, sometimes it takes a very tragic cir-cumstance to get your attention and face what you've done."

"But what is that, exactly? Why do you hate me so much? What could I have possibly done that would make you want to hurt innocent people on your quest to get back at me?"

"You don't remember?" his voice booms. "Let me show you."

The colors on the walls fade, replaced instead by pure dark-ness. Slowly, the darkness gives way to a crystal-clear image, coupled by sounds, smells, and other senses that makes it hard to differentiate between my real vision from what I'm simply viewing.

I'm running. Red lights flash. Sirens blare. The air smells like smoke. Once I get through the crowd at the bottom of the trail, I break into a sprint up the side of the mountain. The oppressive July heat beats down on me but I keep running.

My family is in there. All three of them. My parents were working in the mine when it exploded—no word yet on the number of casualties or who was victim to the blast. Now my little brother is getting ready to run in there.

"All available personnel needed," the voice message read. Sirens have been blaring throughout the city, stopping only to repeat the same message that every firefighter needs to report to the fire in the coal mine.

One foot in front of the other. That's all I can focus on to not succumb to the crippling fear for my family. What if they are all dead? What if in one day I become a brotherless orphan? What am I going to do without them?

Closer to the top of the mountain, I reach the first of the fire trucks, sitting precariously close to the cliff's edge. It doesn't matter. The first responders are so focused on getting everyone in the cave out alive that they don't worry about heights.

Smoke seems to seep from the ground and I cough hard, forcing myself to come to a stop to catch my breath.

"Hey! How'd you get up here?" one of the firemen says to me. "Get back down to the bottom! We don't have the time or the resources to deal with crowds."

"My parents work in the mine," I plead. "My brother's on the department. Arlus Cain. I just signed up myself, too!"

"Your name?" he asks.

"Ash—Ashton—Cain."

"Have you been through training yet?"

Wiping the sweat from my forehead, I buy myself a few extra seconds to come up with the best answer. But my mind is too worried about other things to think up a good lie. "Not yet, but—"

"No 'buts,' kid. This is serious. If you're not properly trained, we can't let you in here. You'd be a detriment to the work that needs to get done. So please, help us by going back down and waiting with everyone else."

"But can't I just sit up here and wait with the survivors? Help pass out water or something?"

"No," he says firmly. "Get back down with everyone who is waiting. We'll get them out as best we can." He waits for me to turn back and head down the path. With no other option, I do.

As I start back, I wrestle with my limited options, trying to talk myself into turning around. Wondering if it'd be better if I just went home like he said. There's nothing but chaos up here. Better to leave the fire department and other first response crews to deal with it all and hope for the best. As much as I hate it, there's nothing more I can do.

Just as I've made my decision to head back and wait it out like everyone else, the ground shakes and I hear people at the top of the path shouting, screaming, yelling at each other to get back, to watch for any flames or hotspots. They call for additional water in the lines. This far up, all they have is the water they were able to load onto the trucks.

Once the ground settles, I sprint back up the hill. The firefighter who stopped me before is gone. Everyone ignores me, too focused on their mission to treat the victims rescued from the mine and to get as many more out as they can.

The smoke gets thicker the closer I get to the top, forcing me to slow down and hook my arm over my mouth to help filter my breaths. Rounding a fire truck, I catch my first glimpse of the entry of the mine. Situated among the rock, it looks like a giant doorframe the way the large wooden beams support the earth above. Smoke billows out of the entry without end, but I know that's where my family is and if I don't try to save them, I'll regret *it for the rest of my life.*

With the cover of the growing smoke, I dart into the cave. Someone sees me outside and calls for me to stop, but I ignore him. The intense hot smoke inside is so thick that I know no one will follow me. It stings my eyes, brings more sweat to the surface of my skin, and leaves me gasping for air, but still, I press on.

The air quality immediately becomes a concern. Even though I hunker low to try to stay away from the majority of the smoke, I still can't get a good enough breath of air. I'm quickly becoming lightheaded. I need oxygen. I should've found an extra mask to bring in here with me.

Keeping my hand against the hot rocky wall, I find a small crevice off to the side and quickly step into it. Thanks to the air-flow out of the cave, most of the smoke passes by and I'm able to catch my breath reasonably enough. Backing away further from the smoke, I nearly stumble into an opening of a cavernous space below. Better watch my feet. I can't see to the bottom so there's no telling how far down it goes.

Crouching low, I breathe in a few breaths that are cleaner than the ones I was breathing before, which isn't saying much. Just as I'm about to begin my descent down the cave again, a firefighter approaches from the main path and catches sight of me. In the full fireman getup, I can't see their face, but they stop and stare at me a moment before stepping toward me.

I consider running further into the cave, but that would burn through the air in my lungs faster and I can't be sure that there will be another crevice like this in time for me to catch my breath. Instead, I sit and wait for the fireman to come closer.

He pulls up his mask and I'm relieved to see it's my brother.

"Ash, what the hell are you doing here? You need to get out of here!"

I open my mouth to protest, but break into a coughing fit. Still, I manage to point to the cavern as a warning.

Chapter Sixteen

"Here." Arlus guides his mask over my face to allow me to breathe.

I suck in the cool, refreshing clean air and my head immediately feels clearer. After a minute, I try to give it back to him, but he puts his hand on my shoulder and keeps the mask on me.

"A few more minutes," he says. "It's not too bad in this crevice, actually." He pulls out a handkerchief and wipes away the sweat and grime from his face. "I'm not even going to tell you how stupid this is. Surely, you understand that, right? It's bad enough I have to worry about finding Mom and Dad and now I need to babysit you too?"

I pull off the mask. "Did you find them?"

Before he has a chance to respond, something explodes again deep in the cave. The ground shakes violently and we both cling to each other, disrupting our balance and sending us falling into the dark cavern.

We land hard on the gravel floor, knocking out whatever air I had in my lungs. I lay flat on my back, gasping while taking an inventory of my body, checking for anything that's broken, bruised, or bleeding.

Sore. Just really sore. That's it.

Rolling to my side, I reach for my brother.

"Arlus," I croak. "You okay?"

Grabbing his thick jacket with both hands, I shake him to wake up. He grumbles and stirs. In the faint light I make out blood trickling from his scalp.

Not good.

"Arlus, wake up." I pat his chest much harder now.

He swats me away. "That was not fun."

Smiling through my relief, I say, "No, it wasn't. And we need to get you out of here." I rise to my feet and tug at his arm in an effort to get him to stand.

He pushes me away. "Stop it. Shh. You hear that?"

I listen carefully, but all I can hear is the ringing in my ears and the shouting of the firemen up at the entry of the cave.

"No, what is it?"

"That hissing sound." He pulls off the straps for his oxygen tank and turns to examine it. "There must be a leak."

"Even more reason to hurry up," I say.

"Hey, is someone down there?" a voice calls from the top of the cavern. I look up and notice it's about a twenty foot drop. Not too far, but still impossible for us to climb without assistance. Or light.

"Yeah, this is Cain," my brother calls up. "And a civilian."

"Are either of you hurt?"

"No," he calls before I have a chance to say otherwise. His head wound doesn't say 'fine' to me.

"All right, just sit tight. We'll do our best to get you out, but first—"

"Got it," Arlus calls to him. "The miners come first. Take your time."

"Why did you say that?" I ask. "You're bleeding, Arlus."

"Because this is all your fault and I want the chance to throttle you without an audience." He marches to me and I creep back, step-by-step.

"My fault? How the hell am I to blame for a natural disaster like this?"

"You're not supposed to be here!"

"I wanted to make sure everyone was safe," I argue.

"No, you wanted to play hero. Didn't want to be overshadowed by your little brother."

"That's not—I didn't know this was going to happen!"

"But you thought you could just walk into a burning cave without any sort of training or protection gear and save everyone single-handedly?"

"I...I...okay, I wasn't thinking," I admit. "I was just...scared. I still am. Arlus, I thought I lost all of you."

"So instead you sacrificed everyone," he says. "I knew exactly *where Mom and Dad were. I was on my way to go get them before I saw you!"*

"So someone else will get them!"

"No one else has that territory! The mine is too widespread. We don't have enough people. They're not going to get to Mom and Dad's territory until all the other ones are cleared. Congratulations! You just sent our parents to their deaths!"

His words hit me like a brick wall. My knees grow weak and I sink to the rocky floor. Even though I had good intentions, I just seriously screwed over my whole family. Instead of me possibly being the only survivor, I've put myself in danger and increased the chances that our whole family is going to die.

"Arlus, I'm sorry. I didn't—"

"Sorry's not going to cut it, Ash. There's no way you can change what you've done. If they die, I'll never forgive you for this."

Rising to my feet, I approach the wall below the opening we fell through. "Come on, if we work together we might be able to get out of here and save them."

"If we get out of here, I'm going to make sure that you're arrested for interfering with a rescue mission."

"Arlus..."

"I mean it, Ash. This is it for us. We're done."

I step toward him and try to put my hand on his shoulder, but he swats it away, followed by a halfhearted push that still knocks me to my feet.

"Hey! Don't act like you're the only one who's upset here!"

"Are you?" he asks. "Because you seem more upset about not being hailed the hero than you do about our parents dying."

"Because we don't know for sure that they're dead!" I shout once I'm back on my feet.

"And we don't know for sure that they're still alive, either!"

Another explosion erupts, followed by the earth shaking again. Rocks tumble from above. The air grows hot. Shouts from the cave call for everyone to take cover. Hurried footsteps indicate firefighters running to safety.

Arlus takes advantage of the distraction to lunge at me, now that he's conceded to the fact that we're going to die. Apparently, he wants to be the one to end my life.

We crash to the gravel beneath us, but before he's able to deliver a good hit to me, a crevice opens up in the rocky wall leading to the path above. Flame consumes my vision until there's nothing left in my consciousness.

Chapter Seventeen
Detective Harkness

Finding parking on Willow Avenue was not fun. The closest spot Detective Harkness could find was two streets over, which, as it turns out, might not be such a bad thing. At least this way she can get a feel for the area and scope out any places Heat might've wandered off to—or been taken.

"Here it is," Perry says to her as they approach Sansone's.

It's a skinny two-story brick building sandwiched between a row of other buildings that are similar in style. Decorative bricks frame an archway over the front door and front window. The front display shows a stuffed brown bear sitting on a camping stool with a fishing pole stuck in painted plastic wrap that's supposed to look like water.

Harkness steps back and eyes up the building from the sidewalk.

"What are you doing?" Perry asks from the door.

"Checking to see if there are any places someone could hide," she says. "The buildings are all side-by-side so it's not like whoever took him snuck from an alley. *If* someone took him."

"His tracer's not working. Someone took him."

"Maybe he just took the suit off," she says.

"And he hasn't picked up his phone?"

"I'm just weighing all the options." She turns and looks to the curb and then across the street. There's a small alley between two buildings across from the sporting goods store, but otherwise the opposite side looks much like this side. "Depending on what time he came, traffic might not have been as busy." She points. "Someone could've gotten him across the street."

"Or *probably* the Gatekeeper sucked him into a portal."

Harkness looks at him. "Oh. Right. That's not the first thing that comes to my mind." She looks up at the second floor. "One of the residents might've seen something too."

"Maybe, but with how close we are to the college, there's a good chance most of the people who live on this street are students," he says. "Which means they *probably* weren't up early enough."

"True. Nobody else would want to live on a busy street like this."

"I'm sure there's *some* people. The artsy people."

"Either way, it's worth checking out if we don't get anything from the store owner. You ready?"

Perry extends his hand toward the entrance. "After you."

A bell over the old wooden door rings when Harkness and Perry step inside. The shop is long and skinny, yet still has enough room to show off fishing poles, kayaks, canoes, even a collection of guns near the ceiling.

To the left is a small wooden counter where two iPads sit. At least there are some parts of this shop that have been introduced to the twenty-first century. But then, to Harkness, she finds small niche shops like this charming, even if it does come with a police headache.

"Can I help you?" someone calls from the back. An older

man wearing a red flannel shirt, jeans, and a John Deere hat.

"Hi," she starts, walking toward him. "I'm Detective Harkness and this is Perry Griswold, we're looking—well, we're looking for Heat." That statement didn't sound as crazy until the words were about to come out of her mouth.

"Heat?" he echoes. "That flaming man?"

Perry smirks and studies the floor.

"Yeah. Red leather suit, throws fire, flies around. He's been on the news."

"I've seen him. Not here," he adds quickly. "No, I've seen him on the news. Why would you think he'd be here?"

"We have reason to believe he wanted to talk to someone here about a case he was following," she explains. "Is there anyone else working or maybe someone different who was working earlier this morning?"

He shakes his head. "No, I'm the only one here and I opened the store."

Harkness and Perry exchange glances.

"What about a man in a leather mask?" Perry asks.

"A leather mask?"

"He's not as well-known to the local media," Harkness adds. "He uses the moniker 'the Gatekeeper.' Leather mask, trench coat, might have some difficulties walking."

The man shakes his head before she can finish talking. "No. Haven't seen him either. I try to stay out of all of that business."

Pulling out a business card from the inside of her jacket, she hands it to the man. "If you think of anything that might help—or if you do see him in the next few days—give me a call on my cell."

"Should I be worried that my store is a target for some kind of criminal activity?"

She shakes her head. "No. Nothing like that. Like I said, Heat was just following a lead on a case and we haven't been able to touch base with him in a while. That's all." Her eyes wander up to the rifles above the shelves. "Your shop I'm sure is perfectly safe."

"I didn't realize Heat was working with the police department—"

"He's not," Harkness says quickly. "It's just a, uh, special circumstance."

"Oh I see. Well, I have security systems and I lock up every night. And the Willow Avenue Business Association is like a neighborhood watch." He follows her gaze up. "Those aren't even loaded! And they're all locked up!"

She smiles. "I'm sure you're very responsible. Anyway, like I said, if you see Heat around here, give me a call."

Outside, Perry says, "That was a bust."

"Not entirely," she murmurs. "We could talk to the residents. Maybe one of them saw something, like you said."

"That seems like a lot of work."

"That's my job." She tries not to think about her suspension. "While we were in there, though, I had another thought. A store like this would probably need to have a loading dock to bring in its larger inventory, right?"

He shrugs. "Yeah, maybe."

"There's an alley out back for local deliveries. I wonder if there's anything out there."

"It's worth checking out."

Walking back to Sixth Street, they find the entrance to the alley behind the shops. This side of the buildings clearly wasn't designed for public viewing. Various additions jut out toward the alley, making some spots pretty tight for a delivery truck to get through. Other stores have a few parking spaces behind them. Most have overhead doors with company logos displayed on them, just like Harkness suspected.

The back end of the sporting goods store is flush with its neighbors. There's a large overhead door and a yellow crisscrossed area on the pavement in front of it.

"What exactly as we looking for?" Perry asks.

"Anything that seems out of the ordinary," she says. "Blood, obviously, but any other signs of a fight too. Weapons, pieces of clothing, glasses, purses, whatever."

"I don't think Heat or the Gatekeeper had their purse with them."

She shoots him a look. "You know what I mean."

"Well, I'm not seeing anything."

Harkness finds a nearby dumpster and peeks inside. Nothing but stuffed garbage bags. She should rip them open to look for clues, but her gut is telling her Heat was never back here.

"Neither am I," she confesses.

"So now what?"

She sighs. "I don't know."

Almost as if on cue, Perry's phone rings.

"It's Rachel," he says before he answers it. "Hello? Yeah, Detective Harkness and I went to Sansone's and we couldn't find anything. Inside, outside, in the back. Nothing." He waits. "Don't you have to work?"

Harkness eyes up the houses on Sixth whose property butts up against the alley behind the commercial buildings on Willow Avenue. Maybe someone in one of those houses saw something. But then, with no evidence that Ash was even back here, there's no reason to waste time interviewing people in the neighborhood.

"All right, we'll be there in a bit," he tells her.

"What's going on?" Harkness asks once he's off the phone.

"She has an idea and wants us to meet at her house."

"What about work?"

"She called in sick. Said finding Ash was more important."

"Can't argue with that," she says. "Let's go."

———

THE GATEKEEPER

HARKNESS PARKS ON the street in front of Rachel's house since the driveway is blocked by a black BMW. Before they get out, they watch the argument ensuing in Rachel's driveway. She and another man that Harkness doesn't recognize. It's not something she usually sees in this neighborhood and not something she's been responsible for clearing up since her uniform days.

"How long were you going to keep this from me?" the man bellows.

"It was only one night," Rachel says. "And he needed a place to stay. What was I going to do? Tell him he couldn't stay here because you're too *jealous* of him?"

"*Is* there something to be jealous about?"

"No! He's just a friend! And if you took the time to get to know him, you'd see that."

"So I have to be friends with all of your friends?"

"Of course not," she says. "But if you're unsure about Ash, maybe you should try to get to know him for my benefit."

"But that doesn't mean that nothing's going on. You could be sneaking around with him when I'm not around. Especially now that he's *living* with you!"

"It's called *trust*, Evan. Try having some."

"You sure you want to walk into this?" Perry asks, pulling Harkness's attention back into the car.

"We're here for a reason," she tells him. "The longer we wait, the longer it takes to find Ash. Who is this guy anyway?"

"Her boyfriend, Evan."

She hooks an eyebrow. "Boyfriend? He's certainly a charmer."

"This isn't his best side."

"I can see that. Let's go."

She and Perry get out of the car and slowly walk toward the house.

"You think I'm a failure because I have less money than I

used to," Rachel says. "Because I value my house over having dinner at the newest fancy restaurants and throwing my name here and there."

"You're just upset because nobody cares about your ordinary, *boring* house or that you're too stupid to find someplace cheaper to live."

"Hey! Hey! Hey!" Harkness shouts as they approach.

The couple finally stops yelling and turns to her.

"Who are you?" Evan asks with venom in his words.

"Oh, so now you care who's listening?" she asks. "You two were just spewing your dirty laundry out for the whole neighborhood to see. Stop it or I'm going to have to take you downtown for disturbing the peace." At his confusion, she adds, "Oh, my name is Detective Jenna Harkness, I'm with the Ellsworth Police Department." They might've taken away her badge and gun, but she's still technically on the force.

His eyes grow wide. "You're a cop?"

"Damn right I am. And I think I've heard enough to tell you that you need to get off this woman's property or I'm going to comb through your history looking for *any* minor infraction to charge you with. So unless you're confident that you have a crystal clear record, I suggest you *grow up*, get back in your fancy little car, and get the hell out of here."

Evan glances to Rachel, then Perry, and finally Harkness. Clenching his jaw, he turns and gets in the front seat of his car. The next moment, he flies out of the driveway and with a screech of his tires, zips down the street, likely to get as far away from his embarrassment as possible.

"I could probably get him for speeding too," Harkness adds with a smirk. "But I'll let it go this time."

"That was awesome!" Perry lets out a hearty laugh. "You *dragged* him!"

"You didn't have to do that," Rachel grumbles. "He was on his way out anyway."

Harkness turns. "I didn't mean to embarrass you. I just don't think that's the way a boyfriend should be acting. No matter how angry he is."

"Let's just get inside so we can talk about Ash. Okay?"

Harkness and Perry follow her through the front door. They each take a seat at the kitchen counter while Rachel moves around on the other side, opening the fridge to bury her embarrassment.

"Can I get you guys anything? Water? Coffee? I think I might have some tea."

Sensing that she needs a distraction, Harkness says, "Coffee would be great if you have it."

"Sure, no problem." Rachel pulls the Keurig away from the wall and unhooks the reservoir to refill it with water. "So no luck down on Willow?"

"No," Perry says. "We even checked around back but there was nothing there."

"The man who opened the shop said he hadn't seen Heat at all," Harkness adds. "Are you sure he went down there?"

"That's where he said he was going." Rachel replaces the reservoir, sets a clean mug underneath the spigot, closes the top, and presses the button to start it.

"And that's where I tracked his last ping before he disappeared," he says.

"Oh, so he *did* go down there?" Rachel asks, hopeful. Beside her, the Keurig groans as the water heats up.

"That's what it looks like, but he never made it inside," Harkness says. "Not according to the shopkeeper, at least. And I don't think he was lying. But kidnapping doesn't make sense because of his powers."

"I suggested the Gatekeeper," he says.

Rachel nods. "That's what I'm thinking too."

"The question is, where?" Harkness tucks her dirty blonde hair behind her ear.

Chapter Seventeen

"That's actually why I called you guys here," Rachel says. "I think the Gatekeeper took Ash to wherever he's been for the last fifty years."

Chapter Eighteen

ASH

"Did you enjoy that little trip down memory lane?" Arlus's voice booms from above me. I'm on my knees, breathing heavy. It's like this place—this bubble—is sucking out every ounce of energy in my body. The painful memories aren't helping.

That's exactly what they are, too. Memories. Now that I've essentially relived them, I remember it clear as day. The double-edged sword decision: stay away from the coal mine and regret not trying to save my family, or run in and get myself hurt in the process.

Either decision was the wrong one. And there's no way I could've ever foreseen the consequences of running in. No way I could've predicted I'd be here—wherever *here* is—with my little brother who is now fifty years older than me and possibly more powerful than I am.

"I think I nailed it right on the head back then," Arlus goes on, "when I told you that you were just trying to play hero. And look at you now! Once again, pretending to be a hero so that everyone can sing your praises."

"I'm trying to help people," I say weakly.

"And what a fine job you've done!" he says with a chuckle. "Tell me, how many people died that day at the coal mine? Did you even care to look into it?"

I don't say anything because I don't know the answer and that would just prove his point. Am I a selfish person for not investigating the coal mine fire more? I was so consumed with trying to remember who I am and figure out how to stop the Gatekeeper and his hitmen that I didn't even really consider the fact that the coal mine explosion took the lives of my parents, among so many others.

But I don't even really remember my parents. Not with my memory still mostly clouded. Was our relationship strained, causing them not to have a significant place in my memories? Or is that part of my brain still wonky from when Arlus and I fell into the cavern?

"You don't know," Arlus snarls. "That day was *my* day to be the hero! It was *my* opportunity to save everyone! And you ruined it! Just like you always did, only this time it cost us our parents. You probably don't even remember them. Not that I should be surprised. You're not as good as everyone here makes you out to be. Trust me, I know how they all bow down for you. But I'm not convinced. In fact, allow me to show you just how horrible you've been in your lifetime."

This memory hits me just as hard as the last one, overloading all of my senses, making it feel like it's happening in real time.

Kneeling on top of a much-younger Arlus, I swing at his face, watching as his cheek instantly starts puffing up from the impact of my fist. He screams for our mother, but I keep going. Pinching him. Pulling his hair. Smacking his face until his cheeks start to turn red. Worst of all, I'm laughing.

"That's what you get for telling everyone at school I still wet the bed," I say.

"Mom! Mom!" he shouts, struggling to push me off of him.

"Hey, what's going on?" She comes into the room and pulls me away from him.

I'm sucked out of the memory quickly and notice Arlus pacing in front of me.

"Finished?" He points at me. "Here's another!"

The summer sun beats down on us, adding to the intense humidity in the air. It just rained and the moisture hasn't been dried up yet. I'm walking through a gravel parking lot, past flagpoles with various flags flickering high in the air. My friends and I dodge the large puddles littering the parking lot. In front of us, a group of younger kids come out of the mess hall.

Summer camp.

I spot my brother and line up my attack. He comes right to me and smiles widely. As he comes my way, I grab him by the shoulder, push him into the nearest puddle and run off with my friends, laughing as we escape inside.

"Not very brotherly of you," Arlus says when I come out of it.

"That was when we were kids." I force myself to meet his eyes. "All brothers fight. That doesn't make it right for you to hold it against me our entire lives."

"All brothers fight, sure, but what exactly did I do to deserve such torture from you?" he asks. "The death of our parents and your simple recklessness was just the last straw for your salvation."

I struggle to stand, but another memory hits me and knocks me to my knees again.

Walking down the hall at school. Arlus's first day in high school. His oversized bookbag trailing behind him, glasses sliding down his nose, at least three zits on his forehead.

"Hey, Ash, maybe you can help," he starts to say as we come closer. "Where's the—"

Chapter Eighteen

Deep in conversation with my friend, I ignore him and pass by without a second look backward.

Later that day, Arlus runs up toward me on the sidewalk, angry.

"I had a great day, no thanks to you," he says.

"What did I do?"

"Completely blew me off earlier!"

"Don't be such a baby," I say. "What were you looking for anyway?"

"Oh, so you did hear me?"

"Kind of hard not to miss the newbies."

"Why do you have to be such a jerk?"

"Why do you have to be such a loser?" I fire back. "Look, whatever it is you wanted to know, you figured it out for yourself, right?"

"Yeah, I guess."

"See? Nothing to worry about."

"Would've been nice to at least have gotten a hello."

"Arlus, if you keep up this whining thing, you're never going to amount to anything. Suck it up and learn to get a thick skin."

I come out of this one but try not to show it. I'm hunched over, leaning on my knees. Those memories ring true in my mind and help fill in the holes that I've been searching for for months. Except, these specific instances don't paint an accurate picture of me and my relationship with my brother. I'm only seeing what Arlus wants me to see. With each new memory he forces on me, ten more come flooding back on their own. Memories that shine a different light on our brotherhood.

"Peanut butter and jelly again?" I ask, pulling out four slices of bread from the bag. Two for me, two for Arlus.

"It's what I like!" he says with a grin.

"If you say so. What else do you want in your lunch?"

"Anything but carrots."

"Celery?"

He makes a gagging sound.

"So not celery?"

"No vegetables."

I laugh. "Deal. But Mom's probably going to make you eat them at dinner."

I made his lunch every day until I graduated high school. And even a few times when I was in college, still living at home, and he was still in high school. We were only a year apart, so the fact that he was my "little" brother faded with each passing year. At one point we simply became "brothers" and the hierarchy we clung to as kids faded. So did any lingering grudges. Or at least I thought.

Apparently, Arlus still clings to that in his senior years. But right now he's just trying to manipulate me. I can't let him. I need to get out of here, which means I need my full strength. Arlus seems to hold all the cards in whatever universe we're in and I think that has more to do with the mind games he's playing on me. Maybe if I focus on the good memories, his strength in this world will subside.

My feet crunch in the snow as Arlus and I walk to the park— bundled up like Eskimos—trailing a single plastic sled behind us. We're about thirteen and fourteen. My friends asked me to come sledding at the park but I told them I was going with my brother instead.

Thanks to the layers we're wearing, we're nearly sweating by the time we get to the top of the hill. Of course, that could also be from the two feet of snow we need to trudge through to get to the top.

"You can go first," I offer.

"You're heavier," he says. "You'll break the trail easier."

"Together?" I ask.

He smiles. "Okay."

I wait for him to climb on, helping him untangle his bulky boot when it gets caught in the rope for the sled. Hopping on behind

Chapter Eighteen

him, I make sure he grabs the rope before I push us off.

The weight of the two of us on the sled sends us flying farther down the hill than the other kids. We both scream as we approach the grouping of trees at the edge of the park, narrowly missing the trunks but slamming into the chain-link fence just beyond. The snow accumulated on the links falls on us as we're sprawled out in the snow.

"You okay?" I ask.

He breaks into a laugh. "That was awesome!"

His reaction makes me laugh too and for a moment, we both just lay in the snow and smile at the adventure.

We were happy. We were friends. Maybe not all the time, but enough not to give Arlus a lifelong vendetta. He's right about one thing: our parents' death was the last straw. Now I'm thinking that straw had nothing to do with me and everything to do with the way Arlus coped with the loss of his entire family in a single day.

I've waited fifty years to realize that my family was dead, initially not remembering who they were to even mourn them. Now that I'm starting to remember, the sadness is creeping in. The longing for something that I don't really remember and what I'll never have again. But I can't think about that right now. I push it away to focus on the current situation: getting out of here.

Arlus, on the other hand, didn't have anything to distract him at the time. Linda said he was in the hospital after the explosion. He had time to think. To stew. To blame me for what happened. He told himself over and over again for fifty years that I was the one to blame for what he'd lost. That if I had just stayed away, he could've saved our parents and kept me alive. As if I single-handedly robbed him of his continued childhood. Eventually, that must've turned into true hatred. Especially with the worry that I might not really be gone.

When he discovered his powers, he must've realized that he

had sent me away somewhere. He must've known that someday I'd return. But it was still a shock when I did. And that reignited his fabricated hatred toward me.

The realization I'm coming to builds a confidence in me. Increases my strength. In this bubble world, my strength dilutes the effect he's been trying to have on me ever since I walked up to Sansone's Sporting Goods and right into his trap. I'm back to full power and my brother is going to pay for what he let his delusions do to so many innocent people.

All at once, my body erupts into flame and I rise in the air. He'll soon know what it really means to feel the wrath of his brother.

Chapter Nineteen
Detective Harkness

And where exactly has Ash been for the last fifty years?" Harkness asks.

"That's the thing we need to figure out," Rachel says. The Keurig to her left stops pouring. She reaches over and grabs the mug and sets it in front of Harkness. "Need anything else with it?"

"No, this is okay."

"So basically we have no idea where Ash is," Perry says.

"You said he just woke up in a cave?" Harkness asks.

Rachel nods. "The old coal mine. And he disappeared the same year of that explosion, so there's a good chance that had something to do with it. Especially since we know the harmful chemicals in the cave are what gave Ash his powers."

"Same with Black Magnet and Dust Storm," he adds.

"And they were hired by the Gate—Arlus," Harkness says. "You know what? I'm just going to use his real name."

"That's no fun," he murmurs.

"Yes, they were both hired by Arlus," Rachel says to Harkness. "Well, probably more like bribed. Arlus definitely had dirt on Black Magnet. And I think Dust Storm was just plain greedy, so convincing him to kill Heat wouldn't have been difficult. Especially once he started digging into the murder of that student."

"Exasperation," Perry corrects. "Dust Storm was trying to help people but he wanted credit for what he was doing."

"Either way, they developed their powers after some sort of interaction with Arlus Cain, right?" Harkness asks.

"Correct. And *the Gatekeeper*," she looks at Perry with a smirk and he fires a finger gun at her, "probably got his powers the same way as Ash did: through the cave."

"What evidence points to that?" Harkness asks.

"How many supers do you see walking around that *haven't* had contact with the cave?" he asks.

"That's speculation," Harkness says. "I'm trying to rely on concrete evidence instead of conjecture. We need to be absolutely sure that Arlus Cain was in that cave and we need to be able to prove that the harmful effects of that cave gave all the supers their powers. If we can't prove that and prove that Arlus Cain has these powers, we don't really have a case against him."

"Well we know for sure that they were in the cave together," Rachel says.

"We do?" Perry asks.

"Yeah." She turns to Harkness. "Ash went to see his girlfriend from 1969 to find out more about himself and one of the things she mentioned was that during the coal mine explosion, Ash and Arlus's parents were trapped inside—"

"Their parents worked there," Perry clarifies.

Harkness nods and turns back to Rachel.

"Anyway, Arlus Cain used to work with the fire department and he was among the people responding to the fire that day."

Harkness's eyes light up. "You're right. That's what his ex-wife said. We can verify all of this with records. This is good. What else?"

"Linda says the last time she saw Ash before a few weeks ago was when he left to run into the mine to save his family," she goes on. "She never saw him after that. Their relationship was serious, too. He wouldn't have just ignored her."

"Yeah and apparently Arlus was the only one of the Cains to be rescued," Perry adds. "And he spent some time in the hospital."

"Right, that's what his ex said too," Harkness says. "Okay, so this helps us try to piece together where Ash might be but doesn't help us put away Arlus."

"Unless you can prove that Arlus has motive to want Ash dead," Perry says.

"But then she would have to prove that Ash disappeared for fifty years without aging a day," Rachel says.

"Yeah, and the former Mrs. Cain told me that Arlus and Ash had 'a normal relationship,'" the detective says. "Like any brothers."

"So…no motive," Perry says.

"Actually, I might have another idea," Harkness says. "I'm working a murder case—well, *was*. Anyway, the victim looked just like Ash and we believe he was really the target based off of the way the suspected killer reacted to Ash when he saw him."

"Donald Douglas?" Perry asks.

Jenna clears her throat, not comfortable sharing details about the case. "Uh. Yeah."

"So what are you thinking?" Rachel asks.

"Maybe I can find a way to prove that Arlus only sent someone after Ash because he looked like the brother he grew up with," she explains. "Of course, that might require involving a psychiatrist to evaluate Arlus, which would require his cooperation."

"That's never going to happen," Perry says.

"No, doesn't sound like it," Harkness agrees.

"Well, it was a good idea," Rachel offers.

The detective takes a sip of her coffee, now only lukewarm. "Good ideas that don't work aren't going to bring Ash back."

"We'll find him," Rachel says. "And I believe we can prove that Arlus has powers through DNA testing. All we'll need is a blood sample."

"You can?" Harkness asks. "That'll require a warrant if he doesn't comply himself, which is unlikely. Still, proving that he has powers doesn't prove that he is responsible for anyone's deaths."

"True," Rachel murmurs. "I just wish we could find Ash. That should be our top priority."

"What if we're not thinking out of the box enough?" Perry asks.

"What do you mean?" Harkness takes another gulp of her coffee. "We're dealing with supers here, I think we're already way out of the box."

"No, I mean with where the Gatekeeper might have Heat," he says. "What if it's not so much a physical place as much as it's an *in between* place."

Harkness hooks an eyebrow.

"Like a limbo space?" Rachel asks.

"Yeah, something like that," he says. "If it really is where Ash had been for the last fifty years, we already know that time doesn't pass there because Ash is still only twenty-two and Arlus is in his seventies. Arlus might've discovered that little trick and now he's using it to his advantage."

"But wouldn't the only way to get there would be through the Gatekeeper's portal?" Rachel asks.

"There could be another way," Perry says. "I just don't know yet."

"This place where time doesn't pass is why I originally thought Ash is where he's been for the last fifty years," she says.

"It would explain why Ash said Arlus seemed surprised when he first encountered him back during the fire storm this summer."

"How do you figure?" he asks.

"Well, if Ash and Arlus got their powers at the same time—back during the coal mine explosion—then maybe Arlus didn't realize he had even opened a portal back then, let alone know where he sent Ash," she explains. "Maybe he tried searching for Ash but couldn't find him and assumed him to be dead. When Ash showed up again—and Arlus had better control of his powers—he resumed the search and found the limbo space."

"That sounds like our best bet yet," Perry says. "And it might even explain what Arlus did to those people who knew about Vernon's accident involving Arlus's daughter."

"You think he put them in the limbo world?" she asks.

"I hope so, but I guess you're right. Arlus isn't exactly shy about killing people."

"True," Rachel murmurs. "It'd be great if we could bring them all home too. But we'd have to come up with some sort of explanation for them losing nearly thirty years."

"Still better than them being dead."

"True," she repeats.

"Okay, we still have another problem," Harkness cuts in. "Where's Joanie Douglas? Would she be with Ash in that limbo place too?"

"Oh," Perry says quietly. "I didn't think about that."

"We'll just have to hope," Rachel says. "Either way, I think the best way to find her is to find Ash, who is probably with Arlus."

"You're right, but the problem still exists," Harkness says. "*If* Ash is in this limbo world, we have no way to reach him without Arlus allowing us in, right?"

Perry sits up. "Actually, I might have an idea on how to get around that." He grabs his keys from the counter and heads to the door. "I'll see you guys later."

"Wait, where are you going?" Rachel calls to him.

"Back to work," he says. "I think I might have something that can get us into the limbo world."

"Do you need a ride?" Harkness calls to him, but he runs out without an answer. "I guess not then."

Rachel pushes the Keurig back to its resting place. Grabbing a dish cloth, she wipes the counter to keep her hands busy. Finding something else to occupy her mind, however, is proving difficult.

"Hopefully he comes up with something," Harkness says.

"Hopefully. The trouble is, even once we find Ash, we still need a case to get Arlus for something. That's where you come in."

"I'm trying." Harkness finishes off her coffee and reaches across the counter to set it down. "If we can get real witnesses to see him unveil himself as the Gatekeeper—or if we can convince a judge to take Ash's statement as Heat—then we won't have any issues proving that Arlus is the Gatekeeper. Then it's just a matter of connecting the Gatekeeper to the crimes, which Donald Douglas has basically already confirmed."

Rachel takes Harkness's mug and puts it in the sink beneath the window. "What if that doesn't work out? You didn't get Douglas's story on record, did you?"

The detective sighs. "No, I didn't. But we'll get Arlus for something. We'll just have to start combing through the records of River Valley Holdings to look for discrepancies or any other illegal activity. It's the same thing that got Al Capone."

"Al Capone didn't have superpowers," she says. "Once we get Arlus behind bars, what's going to keep him there?"

"I guess Perry is working on something that'll dampen his powers," Harkness explains. "I just hope it's finished in time."

"That's a lot of pressure to put on Perry."

"I know, but we need those devices."

Rachel sighs. "Yeah. I just feel…helpless."

"Helpless!? You found where Donald Douglas was hiding out last night *and* you tracked down where the murder weapon was from."

"Ash told you that?"

"No, I figured it out. He's not that good of a liar, but he did try to protect you."

She smiles. "That's sweet. Not that it matters now anyway."

"Hey, we're going to find him *and* give Arlus Cain what he deserves."

"I know. It's just…everything."

"Evan?" Harkness asks.

"Yeah."

"Do you want to talk about it? That fight in the driveway seemed pretty serious."

"No, I'm okay."

"Can I at least say one thing?"

She shrugs in response.

"If someone doesn't respect you now, chances are they're not going to respect you ever," Harkness says. "Think about how long you really think this relationship is going to last if you can't even trust each other."

Rachel folds up the dish cloth and sets it gently on the counter. "I know," she says through a sigh. "But it's…more involved than that."

"I'm sure it's not easy to break off a relationship, but if it's the right thing—"

"I'm pregnant."

Harkness stares at Rachel, completely speechless.

"It's Evan's," she adds, her voice starting to quake. "And it's really bad timing because you're right: this relationship isn't going anywhere and I don't have a lot of money and Ash is staying in my only spare room and I'm not sure I'm going to be able to keep helping him with Heat stuff when I have this baby—*if* I have this baby. It's all just…overwhelming."

"Oh—right, of course it is," Harkness stammers.

Rachel wipes at her eyes. "You probably don't want to hear about it. Thanks for listening to me babble, though. And for what you said outside."

"Of course, yeah. I'm not really good at this stuff, but if you ever want to talk in the future, just let me know."

"Thanks."

"Have you given any thought to what you're going to do?" Harkness asks quietly.

"I don't know."

"You need to tell him." Harkness reaches across the counter. "Only because he's the father."

"I know. But you said it yourself: I can't trust him, which is why I'm stalling."

"How long have you known?"

"About two weeks," she says. "It's been a lot to process. I'm still kind of in denial about it. But I do know one thing."

"What's that?"

"We have work to do."

"Rachel, if you're not up to this—"

"It doesn't matter whether or not I'm ready," she interrupts. "Ash needs us. We gotta save our boy."

Chapter Twenty

ASH

The Gatekeeper's eyes briefly show shock before I tackle him to the ground. He didn't think I'd get back to full strength. Thought his mind games were going to psychologically cripple me.

We collapse backward, me on top of him, still on fire. My hands go right to his throat, just like in the memory. The colors of the walls around us shift from blues and greens to warmer colors. Reds, oranges, yellows. The stronger I feel, the more the walls reflect my power.

Looks like this limbo world isn't solely at the mercy of the Gatekeeper, but whoever is the most powerful. I could use the extra boost.

"Been here before, haven't we, brother?" Arlus snarls beneath me. His voice is contorted as I squeeze his throat.

My burning hands bring blisters to Arlus's neck. He attempts to push me away, but hesitates with the flame.

"Looks like I have to put you in your place one more time," I say.

The Gatekeeper

A portal opens beneath him and he sinks lower, the orb closing before I fall through too. Out of the corner of my eye, I catch the faintest view of the Gatekeeper's boot coming right toward me. There's no time to react before I feel the impact against my side, immediately killing the flames surrounding me and stifling any air that's passing through my lungs. I roll away a few feet and struggle to rise.

The colors of the wall fade slightly.

Arlus gently touches the blisters on his neck, cringing at the pain. "You've always been a bully. Too preoccupied about maintaining your ego at the expense of anyone in your way."

"And what about you?" I fire back, clutching at my side. "You've been so blinded by hate that you've dragged innocent people into this warped sibling envy you have."

"Don't blame me for your shortcomings!" he shouts, rushing to me. The colors of the walls turn a little cooler, hints of greens peek through.

Rolling out of the way, I find my feet and suck in a much-needed breath. Within seconds, I'm ablaze again, hovering in the air. Swinging my arm, I launch my next attack at him. Surprisingly, he chooses to dodge out of the way instead of opening a portal to suck my attack up into.

"What kind of lies have you been telling yourself all these years to continue this manufactured anger toward me?" I ask, still hovering above him.

"I assure you, my hatred it is not manufactured." He watches me from below, moving around so as to never have his back to me.

"Interesting, because after all those other memories you so graciously had me relive—memories that didn't show me in the best light—I remembered more from when we were younger," I tell him.

"How can you be sure your memories are even accurate?"

"How can I be sure that *yours* are?"

Arlus doesn't say anything to that, so I go on.

"We didn't always hate each other. We looked out for each other, even if we weren't exactly friends."

"I know," he says. "That's why for the last fifty years I was hoping you really had died, so it wouldn't have to come to this."

"It didn't have to," I argue. "*You're* the one who made it this way. *You're* the one who brought in other people. And *you're* the reason so many more people are dead!"

"Lies!" he barks.

A portal opens beneath me, putting out my flames, and sucking me in like a vacuum. On the other side, I fall flat on my back in front of Arlus, who steps hard on my chest, pinning me down.

"If it wasn't for *you*, I would've had enough time to save our parents," he says, leaning over me. "*You're* the one who got in the way and thanks to you, I've had to live the last *fifty years* alone!" His foot presses harder against my chest.

"You were married. You had a daughter!"

"And where are they now?" he shouts. "My daughter was murdered and my wife left me!"

Grabbing his foot, I push it away and jump to my feet. He regains his balance and studies me, only a few feet away.

"It wasn't murder, it was an *accident*," I tell him. "And you seemed to have made the most of that situation, or don't you remember how you *used* Vernon Michaels for most of his life?"

"Vernon was collateral damage," he counters. "As you said, simply a way to make the most of a bad situation."

"And me?" I ask. "Was I just collateral damage too?"

He pauses, contemplating. "I didn't know what really happened in the cave until you returned. I figured you were transported through a portal of mine, but I didn't know where I put you. Not until you came back with no memory, that is. And I figured that if I got powers in that cave, then you must've too. That's why I had Vernon work so closely with ESTR, to watch whenever you came back. And security footage for added insurance."

"But it wasn't until *after* I returned that you discovered this place here, was it?"

"It took some time, yes, but eventually I found it."

Looking up, I note how the walls change to deeper, cooler colors again.

"And where exactly is this place?" I ask.

"Does it really exist anywhere? Your youthful appearance and your lack of memory leads me to think that it doesn't. You were simply *paused* in time. Much like the two of us are now. Yet, time still goes on outside. That's why fifty years have been able to go by."

"But you lived those years. You're telling me that after fifty years you're still mad?"

"Our parents are still dead, aren't they?"

"How do you know? What if they went to the same place I did?"

"Look around, Ash!" he barks. "Do you see them anywhere? Besides, the rest of the people in the fire department pulled their lifeless bodies out of the cave while I was sitting in the back of an ambulance getting assistance for *smoke inhalation* and a *bump on the head* instead of helping them like I should've been. If you had just stayed put—"

"So then how do you explain what you did to Vernon? Or Dr. Isaacs? Or Donald Douglas? Or anyone else you hurt or killed along your way for revenge? How do you justify what you did if you thought I was dead too?"

"*Hoped*," he corrects. "I didn't think you were dead because unlike our parents, your body was nowhere to be found, despite the fact that I was standing right next to you when the cave erupted the final time. And because of that slight possibility that you went somewhere, I needed to have…insurances. That came at a cost."

"One that you didn't pay. It wasn't *your* life that you were sacrificing, it was everyone else's. You're a coward, Arlus."

The walls turn nearly black and he lunges at me. I jump back, igniting into flame just as he gets his hands on my throat, squeezing it. Grabbing hold of his arms, I struggle to push him off me, but finally my flames overpower him and he backs away, his arms blistering just as badly as his neck.

All around us, the walls start lighting up, like a rising sun. Taking full advantage of it, I extend my hands toward him and fire a stream of flame at him. He stumbles backward, patting out the flames on his long coat.

The walls burn bright red. I'm in full control now. My powers boosted from being the most powerful one in the room at the time. I wonder if that means the Gatekeeper's powers are dampened because of it.

I strike again before he has a chance to get me, knocking him on the ground this time. He scrambles backward, trips over the length of his coat until he's flat on his back. I stand over him, my burning hand held out above him, ready to attack.

The terror in his eyes stops me and I look at his injuries. *Really* look at them. His neck is red and bubbling with sores. Agitated. Pain that I caused with my own bare hands. That's when I notice his arms too. Just as badly hurt because of the flames—the *anger*—I let consume me while he was physically hurt. I never wanted to kill my brother, only stop him and contain him. By letting myself get this far, haven't I become a reflection of him? I've become the very thing I've been fighting since I woke up from the cave.

The flame surrounding my hand dissipates and I take a few steps back.

Arlus snickers and looks up at me. "Now suddenly you have a conscience? It never bothered you before when you picked on me."

"We were *kids*, Arlus. Let's try to move past that. I'm sorry for running into that coal mine all those years ago. *I* lost *our* parents too. Going in there was a mistake and I shouldn't have done it. But I *did* and there's no changing that."

After all that we've been through since I've been back, maybe a sincere apology is all Arlus is looking for. Maybe acknowledging everything he's been through, including the way I acted when we were younger, is all he needs to hear to end this vendetta.

My gut says otherwise, but it's worth a shot.

"I wanted to be able to save my entire family that day, including you," I go on. "I didn't care who took the credit, I just didn't want to lose everyone. And unfortunately, you're the one who ended up alone and I'm sorry for that. But isn't it time we move past this? Even now, after everything we've done to make each other suffer, I still want to maintain as much of my family as possible. Can't we come to some sort of truce and make amends for what's happened since I've returned? Can we be brothers again?"

Arlus is quiet. He looks away and seems to be considering my offer. There's still a shred of disbelief in my mind, but I want to give him the benefit of the doubt. Maybe he's coming to a realization that all of this fighting is unnecessary. At his age, I'm sure he's thought a lot more about his mortality and the legacy he's going to leave behind than I have. I wonder if the Gatekeeper isn't the image he wants to survive him. I don't blame him for that.

"Okay," he says. "You've got a point." Extending his hand toward me, he says, "Help me up, brother. We're only moving forward from here on out."

With a hint of skepticism, I reach out and grab ahold of his blistered hand, immediately regretting it. A sneer spreads across his face and he yanks at my arm, pulling me toward him. Before I collide into him, another portal opens and we both fall inside.

Chapter Twenty-One
Detective Harkness

Detective Harkness confidently steps off the elevators and into the incident room at the Ellsworth Police Station. She notices her coworkers eyeing her, murmuring to each other. It was only last night that her gun killed a man and she got put on administrative leave.

With her head held high, she marches straight toward Detective Watkins. "I would like to speak with you."

With worry in his eyes, he grabs ahold of her arm and leads her in the direction of the break room. "Are you crazy, Jenna? What do you think you're doing? You're *suspended*. That means no police work whatsoever. And you're even getting paid for this!"

The door to the break room closes shut behind them. "It's not about the money, Walter. I'm here to help close this case."

"Yeah, we're working on it." He looks through the window in the door. "You realize that if Chief Andrews or someone from internal affairs sees you here that you'll be in big trouble, right?"

"Yes, I'm aware, but this case is too important," she says. "Look, I know you and the rest of the team are good at what you do, but you're chasing the wrong lead."

He hooks an eyebrow. "And what lead *should* we be chasing?"

"You need to be looking for a super. One who can open portals and quite possibly even time travel."

Watkins rolls his eyes and steps back, covering his face with his hands. "This is about what happened last night, isn't it?"

"That's not why I'm here, but it does help prove my point that someone with those capabilities is what we're looking for," she says. "I *saw* him, Walt. He killed Donald Douglas. Probably to shut him up from telling us anything else. To prevent us from getting his statement on record."

"Sounds like speculation to me."

"Come on, you don't really think I would shoot a suspect like that, do you? You know me, Walt. The bullets I fired at this super were redirected by him toward Donald Douglas. He wasn't even in range!"

Watkins rubs his chin and squeezes his cheeks before asking, "What makes you think this super knew Douglas told you anything?"

"Because he showed up right after Douglas gave us the whole story."

"Like he was listening in on him?"

"Maybe," she says. "Why? Did you find something?"

"I shouldn't even be telling you this while you're on leave."

"But you know that that's not what happened," she pleads. "Come on, you know me. You know I wouldn't ever intentionally kill someone. This whole suspension is bogus. Now, tell me what you know so I can help you close this case. It's not even about credit anymore. You're the lead, I get that."

He pauses, considering if he should indulge in her requests. "Last night CSI found a bug on Donald Douglas's body."

"I take it you're not talking about an insect."

"No. The lab determined it's a listening device, but they're not sure of the receiver."

"Did you source the bug?"

"Not yet, but it looks custom," he says. "Nothing like what's sold at a store. This thing was smaller than a fly. It's a wonder they even found it."

"So the Gatekeeper was listening in," she mutters to herself.

"The Gatekeeper? You're sticking to that name?"

"Yes, we need to identify who he is. I have a good hunch, but we need evidence before we can arrest him."

"Okay, slow down. This Gatekeeper guy wears a mask, right? He could be anyone."

"Not with his powers."

"Powers?" Watkins says. "Listen to yourself, Jenna. I think the stress of this case is getting to you."

"It's not," she says firmly. "Look, you've seen Heat. You know he has powers and you trust my judgment that he's the same person behind the mask *every* time we see him. Why would the Gatekeeper be any different? Even *if* he puts someone else under the mask for the arrest, we have other evidence that'll show us that, right? Tell me what else you found at the crime scene last night."

Watkins leans back against the table, crosses his arms, and studies her for a moment, wrestling with the decision in his head. "We found some fibers on Douglas."

"Fibers? What kind?"

"Look to be from some piece of clothing. More durable material, so likely something from outerwear or possibly even a pair of shoes."

"Shoes wouldn't make sense," she says. "Not unless he was kicking Douglas, and he showed no sign of any kind of injury like that. Have you sourced the fibers yet?"

"No. But we did find the same fiber in Douglas's jail cell."

"And you *know* that Douglas was talking to someone in a coat right before he disappeared," she says. "We both saw it on the security footage."

He puts up his hands. "I know, I know. It could be from the same coat."

Harkness starts pacing the room, hands on her hips, deep in thought. "It's him, Walter, I'm telling you."

"Okay, so what if it is?" he asks. "What if we really are chasing down a super? How are we going to find him if he can transport himself anywhere? He's already made it clear that we can't contain him. Look at the way he freed Douglas."

"I'm still working on that," she says. "First we need to make sure that we have grounds to even arrest him. Do our duty as cops before we worry about how to keep him there."

"And how do we do that?" he asks. "So far all we know about him is that he has a grudge against Donald Douglas, he might've kidnapped Douglas's daughter, and he has super powers. Not a lot to go on since we can't even verify Douglas's identity."

She stops and looks him straight in the eyes. "All right, I need you to have the guys pull all the records from the Amy Cain accident cases from 1991."

"From 1991? What the hell does that have to do with—"

Harkness puts up a hand to stop him. "Just trust me. I believe it's all connected to the Gatekeeper. I also need you to check with everyone who used to work at the Ellsworth Science and Technology Research lab at the time of the fire to see if they ever took any of their tech home. You found a bug on Douglas that doesn't seem to be from any traditional manufacturer, which makes me believe a place like ESTR produced it. With the recent fire, some of the property might've gotten lost. If I'm right, the bug on Douglas shows the Gatekeeper had access to that kind of tech, so we need to establish a connection."

Watkins exhales loudly, clearly unhappy that she's dishing out orders, but doesn't object any further. "Okay."

"While you're at it, pull out the reports from the Vernon Michaels murder in July."

"That's a cold case."

"Not anymore, I don't think. I also want you to double check with all the area schools, printing offices, teenage hangouts—everywhere you called yesterday asking about Joanie Douglas. Now that we suspect the Gatekeeper is the one who took her, hopefully someone will have seen something."

Watkins shakes his head. "Douglas said his daughter worked at a company that doesn't exist anymore. This seems like a waste of time."

"Oh! That reminds me, make sure you spread your reach out to contacts in 1969. Anyone who used to work at City Print Professionals. I'm talking former supervisors, coworkers, the front clerk, everyone."

"Jenna, this is getting ridiculous."

"Ridiculous or not, Detective, this is now our reality," she tells him. "Donald Douglas said he was from 1969 and we need to believe him. Anything is possible with this super. Besides, everything we've found on Douglas indicates that 1969 is where he belongs. That's the angle we need to follow, no matter how absurd it sounds."

"If you say so."

"Oh, and we'll need to verify his employment in 1969," she adds. "I know he previously worked at Ellsworth Energy, but he told us he worked in planning with the county when he first encountered the Gatekeeper. Call and verify his employment there. I suspect that after Ellsworth Energy started shutting down, he made a career change."

"You better be right about this, because if I start calling and asking for verification from the 60s about a *current* case, you're going to make a mockery out of this department."

"Things are changing, Detective," she says. "Soon the rest of the city will be on the same page as us."

Watkins rises to his feet and steps to the door. "I'll get the crew started on all of this."

"Oh, and one last thing," she says. "I need you to get a search warrant to go through the financial records of River Valley Holdings to see if there's any suspicious activity, specifically when the company first started."

"River Valley?" he asks, confused. A moment later, surprise spreads across his face. "Wait, do you think Arlus Cain is the Gatekeeper? Is that why you want me to look into that case from 1991?"

Detective Harkness stands with her hands on her hips and stares at him, unsure if she should answer. Finally, she says, "We need to consider all possibilities."

"But what is the motive?" he asks. "Why would he want to kill Donald Douglas?"

"Well, once you verify his employment, you'll see that Douglas worked with Arlus's parents at Ellsworth Energy in the coal mines," she says. "There's a good chance he was in the mine during the fire. His survival could be motive."

"A lot of people survived that fire," he counters.

"A lot of people died too," she says. "The Cains among them."

"And your reason for digging up his daughter's accident?"

"Amy Cain was killed by a man named Vernon Michaels, who went on to have an illustrious career at River Valley Holdings, only to die at a River Valley investment nearly thirty years later."

"So?"

"Remember that weird fire storm we had over the summer? The Gatekeeper started that."

"Do you have proof?"

"No, but he was there. Right in front of ESTR."

"Jenna, this sounds like a long shot."

"It's not, just trust me. We have enough to bring him in.

Chapter Twenty-One

When we do, we'll get a confession out of him. I can assure you of that."

Watkins looks at her with skepticism.

"Now can you please get started on that list I gave you? It may take a while. Thank you!"

Watkins shakes his head, but turns and exits back into the incident room to give new orders.

With him gone, Harkness relaxes her assertive stance and lets out a deep breath. She knows she's not wrong about the Gatekeeper, but she just hopes she can prove it with evidence. Without that, they have nothing.

The sudden buzz of her cell phone makes her jump and she quickly pulls it out to answer it.

"Detective Harkness," she says.

"Hey, it's me," Perry says on the other end. "I think I've done all I can do on my Vision Viewer."

"Your what?"

"It's a device that I created to do something else, but significantly tweaked for it to work for us," he says. "It *should* get us to Ash."

"Should? You don't sound certain about it."

"It's never been done before," he says. "So it's risky."

"If it gets us to Ash and the Gatekeeper, it's worth it." She steps toward the door and watches as Detective Watkins talks to the other detectives in front of a white board with important information about the case written on it.

"I agree," he says. "Did you get anything that would give you guys ground to arrest Arlus for any of this? I mean, I want to get Ash back too, but if we can't do anything with the Gatekeeper than this all might just be a moot point."

"I'm working on it," she says. "But you're right. We need to get Ash back. How soon can you meet? We need to move in on the Gatekeeper."

"As soon as you're ready," he says.

"We're going to need backup," she tells him. "If we're going to do this right and get Arlus arrested, we're going to need to do this by the books. That means going into this place that your Vision thing can send us to with backup from the EPD, which means you'll out yourself as Heat's aid to the whole department. Are you ready for that?"

He sighs on the other end. "Yes. And I'm sure Rachel's going to want to help too. We'll do whatever it takes to get Ash back."

"Good. I'll let you know when we're ready. First I need to talk to Chief Andrews."

CHAPTER TWENTY-TWO

ASH

Arlus and I fall from high above the limbo world, which seems to stretch to allow us to descend farther. He really does have control over this place. Luckily, the walls are still burning red, which means I'm the most powerful one in the room.

Wherever we are, gravity continues to be a prominent force and we quickly drop to the bottom. Arlus and I maintain our firm grip of each other's arms, whether out of fear or necessity, I don't know. Despite the inevitable pain I'll cause him, I ignite my whole body into flames to float us down to the bottom to avoid harsh impact.

As soon as the flames arrive, Arlus tries to let go, but I hold onto him tighter until we land. Immediately, he pushes off of me and pats out the flames on his sleeves, grunting at the pain on his arms.

"You really don't care what happens to anyone else, do you?" he asks through gritted teeth.

"I was saving you," I say. "Otherwise—"

I'm interrupted by a portal opening to my right. Arlus is just as surprised by it and it breaks his concentration. When I catch the first glimpse of a police uniform charging through, I pounce on my brother, taking advantage of his moment of weakness to restrain him.

"How did you…?" I gape at the first SWAT officer I see rushing through the portal.

After about ten officers rush in, I see Detective Harkness step through with Detective Watkins, Rachel, and Perry right behind her. Everyone wears a bullet-proof vest. The SWAT team and Detective Watkins wield guns as well.

With the Gatekeeper restrained for the moment and the SWAT team all aiming their weapons at him, Perry rushes up to us and secures a hefty set of handcuffs on Arlus. There's no chain between the links, instead they're held together by a metal box that looks like it contains a battery pack of some sort.

"Power dampener," he explains. "I have it set on high so he actually shouldn't have any use of his powers."

Two SWAT officers step up and each grab one of the Gatekeeper's arms, immediately pulling off the leather mask. Arlus's wispy white hair falls in his enraged face.

"Arlus Cain!?" one of them says.

Detective Harkness steps up to him defiantly and says, "Arlus Cain, you're under arrest for the murder in the first degree of Donald Douglas, murder in the second degree of Peter Jones, the kidnapping of Joanie Douglas, and I'm sure so much more. Watkins, why don't you read him his rights and we can get the hell out of here?"

The rest of the SWAT team forms two human walls so that Detective Watkins and two SWAT officers can lead my brother back through the portal.

"Arlus Cain, you have the right to remain silent…" Watkins starts. As they exit into the portal, the rest of the SWAT team follows, leaving me, Harkness, Rachel, and Perry all alone.

"We did it," Harkness says to me with a smile. She looks around and adds, "But where the hell are we?"

"Arlus's own little dimension," I answer quickly, before pointing over to the side. "Joanie's here too."

Rachel rushes over to her and checks for a pulse. "She's breathing, but it's very faint. We need to get her to a hospital for a full evaluation."

Perry and I run over to help lift Joanie and carry her to the portal.

"How'd you guys get in here?" I ask.

"You know how I finished the Vision Viewer?" Perry carries Joanie's legs in his arms. "I modified that to allow us to actually *transport* ourselves to our vision."

"It was very hypothetical," Rachel adds. "We kind of manufactured a vision in our own heads of where you were so we could travel here."

"Well, *she* manufactured the vision," he corrects. "She focused on you and thought about what this place might look like."

"So there was only a slim chance you'd actually find me?" I ask, keeping a firm grip under Joanie's arms. Only a few more steps to the portal entrance.

"Yeah." She looks down at her feet as she follows us.

Must've been a pretty strong connection to me then.

"Let's continue this conversation back in the real world," Harkness says. "Ready?"

"More than ready," I say.

Perry and I step through the portal first with Joanie Douglas supported between us. On the other side, we step out into the open incident room at the Ellsworth Police Station downtown. Throughout the room, officers watch with wide eyes as we each appear through the portal. No sign of the SWAT team or Arlus Cain, which must mean that they took him straight to an interrogation room.

THE GATEKEEPER

The blinding sun shining through the windows across the room tells me it's early evening. I spent a whole day with Arlus in his own little world—literally. But it's over now.

Perry sets Joanie's legs down on the floor and I lower the rest of her body down too. He steps over and turns off his modified Vision Viewer once we're all through the portal. Rachel steps to take his place by Joanie and says to the room, "Call an ambulance! We need to get her checked out right away."

Two officers spring forward and lift Joanie up, carrying her toward the elevators. Rachel follows them and pulls out her phone to call the ambulance herself. Luckily, we're already downtown so Ellsworth General Hospital isn't too far.

"I'll go make sure they're okay," Perry murmurs and exits the room toward the elevators.

Among those watching our return is a man in a navy blue suit. He has thick buzzed gray hair and tan skin with several wrinkles. The same man I saw at EIT just before I captured Dust Storm.

When the commotion subsides, he steps forward and extends his hand to me. "Heat? I'm not sure if you remember, but I'm Ellsworth Police Chief Jackson Andrews. Nice to see you again. I want to thank you for all you've done for the city. If you have the time, I'd love to sit down with you in my office to discuss things further."

I look over to Harkness for any sign of what he's talking about, but she shrugs, unsure herself.

"Uh, yeah," I stammer. "Okay. Right now?"

He holds up a finger toward me and turns to Harkness himself. "Detective Harkness, I'm surprised to see you here."

Panic fills her eyes. "Sir, I know I'm not supposed to be working, but in all fairness, we got the suspect in custody and—"

"I know," he says. "And as far as I'm concerned, right now you're just visiting your coworkers."

She smiles. "Yes, that's right."

"However, I think internal affairs would be interested to know about this new development in the case," he goes on. "By that I mean, the *super* we have in custody. I think it's safe to say that most of the department has been turned into believers after today."

There are sniggers from all around the office. Charging through a portal to arrest a man in a mask probably wasn't the first thing everyone thought of accomplishing this morning.

"It's hard to ignore their existence now," he says. "I will personally see to it that internal affairs takes this arrest into consideration when evaluating your case. I suspect your employment will be reinstated as soon as possible."

"Thank you, sir!" she blurts with an even bigger smile on her face.

"All right, you should get out of here," Andrews tells her. "I think Detective Watkins can finish up." Turning, he looks back at me and says, "Let's head up to my office, shall we?"

He leads me down a hallway with a window overlooking St. Mary's Church at the end. Stopping at a door right beside the window, he unlocks it and swings it open for me to step through.

"First off, I want to apologize for the way I acted during our first encounter a few weeks ago." Andrews closes the door after we step in. "At EIT. To be honest, I was worried because the department had never faced anything like that before—with the supers, I mean. It was, uh, eye-opening."

"It's okay. I understand."

"Thank you for that." He motions to a pair of chairs near his desk. "Please, have a seat." As he moves to his side of the desk, he says, "So you got the Gatekeeper then, huh?"

"Yes, sir."

Once he's seated, he says, "I understand that a few friends of yours helped ensure the safe arrest of our suspect."

"Uh, he—um."

Andrews smiles. "Perry told us himself earlier today. That

girl too. Uh…Rachel's her name, right?"

"Yeah."

"They were quite concerned about finding you and stopping the Gatekeeper. Turns out your friends know a thing or two about things we as a department need to learn."

"Yes, sir," I say. "They're very intelligent."

"As I've seen, yes. However, in the rush of trying to catch our suspect, nobody was able to get their full names or contact information and I'd like to stay in touch with them for future developments in technology. Once again, with the rescue of another victim, they were unable to disclose this information. I was wondering if you would be able to provide that."

"Sir, with all due respect, I'm not sure if I feel comfortable with that."

"I understand," he says. "Believe me, if you don't tell us, we'll find a way to track them down and get in touch with them. I just thought that it'd save time and would help us get up to speed with these supers faster."

"What exactly do you have in mind for them?" I ask.

Andrews leans forward on his desk, the tips of his fingers touching his chin. "Since the capture of Dust Storm, we've been discussing the need to update some of our jail cells to accommodate criminals with powers, as Perry's just done with the Gatekeeper."

"Well, it sounds like he's your guy. He's working on trying to implement his tech so that the prisoner's powers will be dampened in a room, which would mean he doesn't need to wear the handcuffs all the time."

"Like I said, we'll have to get in touch with him. And your other friend. But for the moment, what I also want to talk to you about is first and foremost to thank you again for doing your part to protect this city. Obviously, you've been granted certain *capabilities* in your powers that no one in this department—to my knowledge—possesses and it's very admirable that you've decided to do something good with what you have to offer because as we've both seen, there are others who have not chosen to follow the same path."

I smile, but with my mask he can't see. "Thank you, sir. It's definitely nice to hear that what I try to accomplish doesn't go unnoticed, but please know that I don't operate alone. Albeit small, I have a support team behind me that backs me up during my inevitable shortcomings."

"You're only human—rather, that's how I'm going to proceed. You're bound to have shortcomings, but it's not those shortcomings that bring fault, it's the inability to recognize them. You've recognized your weak points and have done what you can to assemble a team whose strengths are your weaknesses. That's a sign of a real leader. Actually, that's a trait we look for in every Ellsworth Police Officer.

"Your contributions to this city and the safe arrest of the Gatekeeper this evening are primarily the driving factors behind my decision to campaign for a Supers-Related Homicide Unit, which would handle all future cases regarding supers. These... *beings*, like yourself, are unlike anything we've ever seen before and we need to be prepared for them."

"And they can be dangerous," I add. "At least, the ones we've encountered."

"And I'm sure there's more," he says. "Regardless, we're just happy that we seem to have one of these supers on our side. I've been made aware that Detective Harkness has already determined your value to us and some of our investigations as an informant. In an effort to make sure you're fully aware of our intent to treat you as an honorary member of law enforcement, I'd like to extend an offer to have you take an oath and officially join our new Supers-Related Homicide Unit."

"You want me to become a police officer?" That's what my plans were in 1969, according to Linda. Maybe everything is working out the way they were supposed to.

"Not an official police officer, per se," he corrects. "If you want to maintain your identity, you won't be able to be fully admitted to the force. However, the oath we'll have you take will be modified to fit your situation but will keep you obligated to maintain the same standards as every other member of the Ellsworth Police Department. You would be included in investigations related to supers and it would be your duty to keep the unit updated about any potential threats you see arising. Do you understand?"

I smile again and nod. "Yes, I do. And I accept—well, wait a minute. What's the pay like? Because becoming an honorary member is great and all, but unless it can pay my rent it's not going to last long."

He laughs. "We can discuss a salary. But beyond that, I wanted to also talk to you about this team you mentioned. A lot has happened in the past few months and you and your team have handled much of it. It's impressive and, once again, something we look for in people to join the force. I've assembled a list of detectives who might be interested in joining this new unit—Detective Harkness at the top of that list—however, we need people specialized in things outside of our current capabilities."

"You mean Perry and Rachel?"

He nods. "I promise to keep the names of your team between us unless they say otherwise, but I'd like to offer them an opportunity to work with the same unit, similar to what I've presented to you, depending on their skillsets."

Letting out a deep breath to buy time, I consider my options. Perry already has a job he likes, but he's also been developing tech that I've used that's helped me as Heat. If he could continue to do that—and get paid for it—then maybe that wouldn't be such a bad gig for him.

And Rachel doesn't really even like her job at the hospital, but maybe the police could offer her an opportunity to study supers and how they develop powers. Of course, that could very quickly get her involved in classified federal work and I'm not sure that stress is something she'd want to take on.

Of course, both Perry and Rachel are grown adults. As Chief Andrews said, they can both make the decision for themselves once the offer has been extended.

"Well, Perry's last name is Griswold," I start. "He's currently employed at the Ellsworth Institute of Technology in one of its science buildings."

Andrews writes down the name on a pad of paper in front of him and listens as I recite his phone number. "And Rachel's?"

"Um…it's Rachel Chandler."

"And what does she do right now?"

"Well, right now she works at Ellsworth General as a Lab Technician. But she's the one who first ran tests on me to see what gave me my powers and she even figured out the source of it too."

Andrews's eyebrows go up. "You know what gave you your powers?"

"Yes, but that is all in her research," I say. "Some of it she's had to redo since her files were lost in a fire."

"The Ellsworth Science and Technology Research fire, right?"

I clear my throat. "Uh, yeah." How does he know that?

"I've done some preliminary research on you as well," he says with a smirk. "A building burns down in a fire and a flaming man flies toward it. Even you would have to admit that it raises suspicion. But I'm sure you had nothing to do with that."

"No! And neither did Perry or Rachel. That was Arlus—the Gatekeeper."

"I look forward to hearing all about your trials and tribulations as Heat, but I think it's probably better if we wait until you're an official member of this team, don't you?"

"Uh, yeah. I guess that's probably best."

He smiles at me again. "I'll track down your friends and see what they have to say. Does Detective Harkness have a way of getting in touch with you?"

"Yeah, she does."

"Perfect. I'll have her contact you once we figure out all of this administrative stuff. In the meantime, I'm sure you're not going to stop being Heat."

"No, sir."

"Good." He stands and extends his hand again. "I look forward to working with you."

———

AFTER MY MEETING with Chief Andrews, I head over to the room marked OBSERVATION ROOM #4. Detective Harkness is here with the transcriber and Officer Lawson, who studies me when I enter.

In the corresponding interview room, Arlus sits in his Gatekeeper suit sans mask. His neck and arms are smeared with an ointment, but otherwise no other first aid treatment has been administered. He probably denied it to keep some semblance of his pride. Opposite him sits Detective Watkins. Arlus looks tense. Annoyed. Angry, more like it. It only makes me more smug.

"Hey," Harkness murmurs as she gets up to join me from her seat by the transcriber.

I stand beside her and watch as Watkins makes further notes in Arlus's growing file. Neither of them saying much on the opposite side.

"Anything?" I ask.

"Not at first," she says. "We found a listening receptor in his coat pocket that we believe is linked to the bug we found on Douglas's body. That's probably how he was listening in to our conversation last night."

"He probably had a bug on all of his hitmen," I add.

"Quite possibly. We also found the photo of Joanie tied up in his coat pocket. The one he probably showed Donald Douglas to bribe him."

"Well that proves that."

"Yup. And it was hard for him to deny the fact that he's the Gatekeeper, so he already signed that confession. Plus, we have CSI testing the fibers from his coat with the ones found at the crime scenes and we suspect they'll match."

"Good, but that still doesn't conclusively mean he killed them, does it?"

"No, that's what Watkins is working on now."

I keep my eyes on Arlus. "I'm guessing from the silence, he's not admitting anything more, is he?"

"Well, he hasn't invoked his right to counsel yet, so we need to tread carefully," she says. "Hopefully we can get a confession before he calls a lawyer."

"Hopefully."

"So tell me about your relationship with Vernon Michaels," Watkins says on the other side of the glass.

Arlus shrugs. "What do you want to know?"

"Well, it's more than a little unusual that the man who hit and killed your daughter suddenly became a lifelong employee of yours."

"Keep your enemies close."

"So you considered Mr. Michaels an enemy?"

"He killed my daughter."

"Yes, I know." Watkins sorts through the papers in the folder in front of him. "And then all the responding officers, medical professionals, and prosecutors involved in the case mysteriously vanished in the following months. I'd say that's highly suspicious, don't you?"

"Are you trying to indicate something, Detective?" Arlus asks.

"Based off of your *unique* abilities, it poses the question:

did you have anything to do with the disappearances of those people?"

Arlus smirks. "Debt is a funny thing, isn't it? When you lose someone, everyone rushes to help. Sure, the person responsible might go to prison, but it doesn't *really* help you cope, does it? The debt never *truly* repaid. So I viewed my daughter's death as an opportunity."

"To do what?" Watkins asks.

"To make sure that the man responsible continues to pay that debt he owed me for as long as I saw fit."

"You're talking about Vernon Michaels."

"If he went to prison, he wouldn't have been able to do everything I asked of him," Arlus goes on. "It's because I seized the opportunity that I enjoyed a long career as the head of my own company."

"So in order to blackmail Mr. Michaels, you got rid of everyone who was trying to let our justice system do its job because you wanted him to be indebted to you."

"Ah, you've figured it out," Arlus says with an arrogant smile.

"Just for the record, what did you do with those people you 'got rid of'?"

"Let's just say, I guaranteed that they'd never become an issue again."

"So you killed them?"

"When was the last time you heard from them, Detective?" he asks with a sneer.

"He's not answering the question," I say.

"He's said enough," Harkness assures me. "Watkins will get him. And he wants Arlus to admit that he redirected my bullets toward Donald Douglas too."

"At least some good will come of this," I say.

"More than some," she says. "We got him. Watkins will keep working on him. Arlus is full of himself. With some prompting, he's not going to be able to hold back talking about himself and everything that he's done. Now we just need Perry to get to work on a prison cell that can hold him. For now, though, the handcuffs will work."

"Definitely," I say, staring into the next room. I thought I'd feel a better sense of accomplishment now that Arlus is arrested, but instead it just fuels me with even more reason to continue working as Heat. If another super comes along who does only a fraction of the damage that Arlus has done, it'll still be too much. "We don't want to let him go."

Chapter Twenty-Three

ASH

We all raise our drinks in the air over the table and clink them together.

"To Heat, for successfully bringing the Gatekeeper to justice," Harkness says.

"And to you, for rejoining the force," Rachel adds, raising her glass of water. "Congratulations."

"Not official yet," she corrects.

"But it will be," Perry says.

"And it wasn't all me who caught the Gatekeeper," I say. "Actually, I would even say that it mostly *wasn't* me."

"True, we did most of the work," Harkness says, breaking into a smile at my shock.

"So the police decided to listen to a masked vigilante?" Perry asks.

"He won't technically be a vigilante for long." Harkness takes a sip of her beer.

"Yeah, how did you manage a sweet deal like that?" he asks.

I motion to myself. "Is it a crime that someone acknowledges my talents?"

"Oh God," Rachel groans.

Harkness rolls her eyes.

"They must acknowledge mine too because I already got a call from someone at the department who wanted to talk to me about potentially working with their engineers for a super prison," he says. "Well, a prison for supers."

"We got it," Harkness says.

"You already got a call?" Rachel asks, surprised.

After I left Chief Andrews's office, I met up with Perry and Rachel at the hospital and told them everything about the Supers-Related Homicide Unit. They were waiting for Joanie to be stabilized. When she's released in the next day or two, we'll get her set up with a new life here. Perry's tech might've gotten them to Arlus's limbo world, but it's probably not advanced enough to send someone back in time. Nor would any of us feel safe with that type of technology in the world.

"I gave the police your information too," I assure her. "Chief Andrews seemed very interested that you figured out how all the supers got their powers."

"Yeah, but I haven't heard anything yet."

"It's still early," Harkness tells her. "They literally just talked to Ash a few hours ago. I'm surprised Perry got a call already."

"Well, containing a super prisoner is kind of a pressing concern now that they have the Gatekeeper," he says.

"True." Harkness tips her bottle toward him.

Rachel wipes away the condensation at the bottom of her glass without saying a word.

I tap her on the arm and say, "Why don't you come up with me to get some more drinks?"

"We just got some," Harkness says quickly. "And I thought Rachel said she wasn't going to drink tonight?"

Grabbing my bottle, I down it until it's gone and let out a

loud belch. "All gone."

"Subtle," Perry murmurs.

Rachel rolls her eyes and gets up from her seat. "I can help you get more."

We both walk up to the bar and I order another round of drinks for everyone. When the bartender steps away to grab them, I tell Rachel, "I wouldn't worry too much about not getting a call yet."

"Easy for you to say."

"Yeah, because I just stumbled into this job my first day out of the cave. Rach, for me this is the break I've been waiting for. And I did what I could to make sure you and Perry could cash in on it."

"I know," she says. "And I don't mean to rain on your parade. It's just…not really been a good day."

"Scared I was going to get stuck in there, were you?" I ask with a smirk.

She rubs the back of her neck, studying the sticky bar top. "Yeah, I suppose."

My face drops and she catches my look out of the corner of her eye, doing a double take at my disappointment to her lack of enthusiasm.

"I mean, yeah, of course I was," she corrects. "That's just not what's on my mind right now."

"What is it then?" I ask.

The bartender comes back over with fresh bottles and collects my money. The allowance Perry gave me when we came in. It's basically already gone. Luckily, I won't have to keep borrowing money from everyone once Heat is officially part of the Ellsworth Police Department and is receiving a paycheck.

"It doesn't matter," she says. "I'm not trying to spoil the evening, so I'll suck it up."

"Rach, if they don't call you, Heat will be bringing up your name over and over again until they're forced to call you about something. I'm not going to let this go. You helped a lot on this case. You found out where Donald Douglas was hiding and you sourced the murder weapon. *And* you helped get Joanie to the hospital as soon as we got back. That was all you. Not to mention everything you've done for me—and by extension, the city—since I walked down from the cave."

"Yeah, I know you're right." She uses a cocktail napkin to wipe away the condensation rings on the bar top.

"Besides, even if the police *don't* call you, with everything you have to offer, something is bound to turn up in the future. Your job at the hospital isn't permanent unless you say it is."

She looks at me and smiles, then leans up and kisses my cheek. "I love how sweet you are."

I can't keep the grin off of my face. "What was that for?"

"Just cause," she says with a shrug.

"Isn't Evan going to get jealous?"

"Oh, you didn't hear, did you?"

"Did you guys break up?" I ask a little too fast.

"No." Rachel gives me a look. "But he *did* find out that you're living with me now."

"One night means we're living together?"

She looks at me again. "We both know it's going to be longer than that."

I offer a smirk. "What did he say?"

"Well, he wasn't happy. We got in a fight, which carried outside. Detective Harkness had to break it up. That was earlier this morning. I haven't talked to him since."

I look over at Perry and Harkness talking back at our table. She looks up, smiles, and offers a little wave. Her actions are almost in complete contrast of the hard exterior she puts on at work. More vulnerable. Like she was last night when she kissed me. And I still don't know what to make of that. Especially now that Rachel's essentially telling me that her relationship with Evan is at the beginning of the end.

"Is it going to be a problem when we go back to your place?" I ask.

"No," she says definitively. "It's my house and I get to decide who can stay there. I'll think about it tomorrow. Right now, we said that we're going to celebrate everything you and Detective Harkness have accomplished. I'm proud of you, Ash."

"Thanks," I say. "That means a lot. But it's what we've all accomplished. I couldn't have done this without you and Perry. Especially you."

"Who else would you complain to when you're mad at Perry?"

I laugh. "That's true."

She nods back to our friends. "What do you say? Think it's time we rejoin the others? I'd say there's still a bit of celebrating left."

"We've only just started."

Ethan Pierce is just another IT tech support rep at Wyatt Industries until he's zapped and infused with enough electricity that should kill him. But electrocution has just given Ethan terrifying abilities that no man has ever had.

As he grapples with his strange new powers, he and his girlfriend Emma witness a drive-by shooting in the city of Olympia. They soon learn it was related to the Martelli crime family that run the city and don't like to leave loose ends.

Fearful of the threat of the family, Ethan and Emma try to lay low, but it's no use. When Emma is attacked, Ethan uses his newfound lightning abilities to become Fuse, Olympia's "man in black."

Fueled by vengeance and empowered by his new abilities, Ethan vows to find the man who attacked Emma and get justice. But will his powers be enough to save her?

———

Available in ebook, paperback, and audio!
DavidNethBooks.com/Fuse

More by the Author

To find the rest of the author's books visit
DavidNethBooks.com/Books

Subscribe to his newsletter to be the first to know of new
releases and special deals!
DavidNethBooks.com/Newsletter

If you enjoyed the book, please consider leaving a review on
Goodreads or the retailer you bought it from. Reviews help
potential readers determine whether they'll enjoy a book, so
any comments on what you thought of the story would be very
helpful!

About the Author

David Neth is the author of the Heat series, Fuse series, the Under the Moon series, and other stories. He lives in Batavia, NY, where he dreams of a successful publishing career and opening his own bookstore.

———

Follow the author at

www.DavidNethBooks.com
www.facebook.com/DavidNethBooks
www.instagram.com/dneth13